Macca Tree
Manns

Macca Tree Manns

ADDEAH PALMER

IAN RANDLE PUBLISHERS
Kingston • Miami

First published in Jamaica, 2015 by
Ian Randle Publishers
11 Cunningham Avenue
Box 686
Kingston 6
www.ianrandlepublishers.com

NATIONAL LIBRARY OF JAMAICA
CATALOGUING-IN-PUBLICATION DATA

Palmer, Addeah
    Macca Tree Manns / Addeah Palmer

      p. ; cm
ISBN 978-976-637-892-9 (pbk)

1. Jamaican fiction   I. Title

813   dc 23

Cover and Book Design by Ian Randle Publishers
Printed and bound in the United States

For Nell

Macca Tree

Pretty Rose got Macka Jook
So don't get too close when yuh a look
Admire di beauty but careful wid wha yuh a duh
Cause everyway yuh tun Macka Jook yuh

–   Addeah Palmer

Contents

Acknowledgements

I would like to express my profound gratitude to all those who supported me throughout the writing of this book.

I am deeply indebted to my mentor, Ms Jenni Campbell, without whom this novel would have never been written. I would also like to pay tribute to Ian Randle Publishers for publication; humblest gratitude to those who assisted in the editing, proofreading and design.

I would like to extend special thanks to my friends and family members who supported and encouraged me on this journey.

Above all, I thank God through whom all things are possible.

1. Return of the Manns

No one knew exactly when Gloria and Kenneth Mann arrived in Macca Tree, in Westmoreland. One usual unaccounted-for morning, everyone woke up and they were just there, settled in an unfinished, precarious, lopsided board house in an overgrown square of land that even the stray dogs ignored.

Macca Tree, a sleepy farming community, buried under acres of sugar-cane land, never buzzed, except for the loud and flamboyant church crusades that seemed unending under a green and white striped tent, pitched by Pastor and his faithful flock.

Pastor's crusades attracted many from outside the community. Some would travel for miles on foot or bicycles just to see the miracles unfold. Pastor's buxom wife, Monica, 'getting into the Spirit' was an attraction all by herself, ready to be marketed.

The community was self-sufficient. Apart from Pastor and his flock, there was an upscale brownstone concrete church, which hosted a school during the week; a family-run supermarket; two bars and six shops. Macca Tree stretched for nearly three miles over a few hills, around some deep corners and lay smack in the middle of two other communities – the nondescript Top Road and the ghetto splattering called Bottom Road.

The pride of Macca Tree was the asphalt road which ran the spine of the community, contrasting with the lush green lawn grass on each property, and made for easy commute. The road brought residents together and kept them apart. They maintained a road-cleaning regiment with military precision by taking turns to sweep it every morning, rain or shine. Except for a disorderly pack of stray dogs that half-yearly increased their number, nothing else was allowed to disfigure the pride in the well-kept street.

Board houses painted in vibrant colours gave life to Macca Tree outside of Pastor's crusades. Among the kaleidoscope, there was a single concrete, white house, jailed by whitened steel grilles, belonging to Tom McEnuff and his generations who owned the majority of the sugar-cane fields in Macca Tree, which supplied tonnage to the nearby Frome Sugar Factory.

The McEnuff's contribution to the road was a grilled fence with automated gate. This added much to the whispered curiosity of Macca Tree residents, as it was the crowning glory among the neatly lined out barbwire fences supported by posts cut from trees in the community.

Farming was the profession of choice; acres of cane fields, three-month cash crops and year-long yam and potato investments occupied the second-tier pride of place and determined class and respectability. Big yards boasted a wide variety of mango, orange, plum and other fruit trees, making a blooming orchard of the community. Macca Tree was their little piece of heaven and the residents were fiercely protective of their community.

Enter Kenneth and Gloria Mann, with a history rooted in family, noise and disturbance. It was not pleasant. A regular uneventful Macca Tree morning was about to get prickly.

On that bright Saturday morning as the sun peeped through cracked clouds, the smells of homemade sweet potato pudding played with the nostrils of the Mann family who stood facing the house which had not been inhabited for more than three years. The once-painted walls of the six-room house at the end of the Road were now old and cracked. The crookedness of the structure told tales of woe and possession by uncaring tenants. The few window panes that withstood the trauma of time, nature and neglect clung clumsily to their frames, twisted and caked with dust and decay. Gaping doorways where doors once hung added to the desolate aura of the house.

As if in anticipation of their arrival, the stray dogs kept the community awake the fateful night, barking at shadows, fighting and prodding over bitches in heat. A clear signal of what was to come, a single black mongrel covered in mange, found comfort on the steps leading to the house they were to occupy, next to the front yard of respectability and class, beside the epitome of good grace and the aspiration of Macca Tree itself; they were neighbours, immediate and unrepentant to the McEnuffs.

The interior of the isolated house was throttled by Anansi web stringing from the ceiling to the floor – not even the forceful breeze from the Caribbean seashore could penetrate the thickness of the woven snare. Dust danced in the ray of sunlight which played peek-a-boo with the holes in the wall. The stale air and the unstable wooden flooring completed the ghastliness. But the Manns settled in comfortably and contentedly.

They set up a clothes line across the front yard and Gloria spared no time in hanging out the clothes she had washed on arrival. In the bundle was Kenneth's work pants that bore the strains of his mistakes and her efforts at patching to correct them; drawers that had seen too many years and shirts heavy with stain that retailed bleach could not remove.

Gloria hummed as she worked. *"What a frien' we have in Jesus...hmmmm, hmmm...."*

Kenneth, armed with a machete, was in full attack of the overgrown grass as if it had done him serious harm.

Ms Joyce, who lived across the road, was out early to perform her street-sweeping duties. "Lord Jesus Christ Gloria! Is when unoo come?" she peered over the fence, looking past the string of clothes.

She did not wait for an answer, as she shouted: "Georgie, Maas Joscelyn, unoo look yah nuh!" Kenneth raised his head at the sudden disturbance. "Lawd man, unoo nuh badda with the excitement. We just come to wi yard and nothing nuh wrong wid dat."

Gloria interrupted her clothes hanging, placed her hands akimbo, and readied herself for the usual tracing match to which she has been the undefeatable champion from primary school. "Why yuh calling down crowd on wi?" She demanded. "We come back to Macca Tree, we don't want any trouble."

The noise had gathered the residents into a huddle across from the Manns' new place of abode. Ms Joyce, the head cheerleader of the commotion, spoke while adjusting her black and white polka dot head tie. Hailed as the mother in the community, she took her role seriously enough to greet Gloria with a loaded mouth.

"So is what breeze blow you back to Macca Tree, Gloria? We thought you left for good last time," she moved to the gate to get a closer look at the spectacle of the Manns.

"Don't worry 'bout we Joyce, we quite fine. Stop put mi business pon shout and just mind your own."

But Ms Joyce would not let up.

"Is a simple question mi ask you Gloria. Why you must always ready fi a fight?" Ms Joyce countered.

Gloria returned to her clothes hanging, bent over the half-empty basin of fresh wash and hoisted her backside in the air towards the enthralled crowd.

"Well I never tell you fi move your foot mek mi put in mine; you cyaa finish it, nuh start it Joyce."

Never one to pursue the likes of Gloria, Ms Joyce retreated. That's a fight she could not win even on a picture-perfect day like today; she knew based on past experience that like a ship among toothed rocks in the ocean she would be chewed up and spat out in pieces, courtesy of Gloria. With her surrender, the curious crowd returned to their business, clobbering Gloria's name in the process.

Kenneth stopped wrestling with the uncooperative weed long enough to speak.

"Gloria, I thinking of asking Mr McEnuff for a job. What yuh think?"

"I think wi gonna have a problem wid these people in Macca Tree. The gall of them to seek an explanation for wi return."

Kenneth hung his head knowing there would be no answer from his wife when she was up in arms. He shrugged his shoulder and resolved to continue cutting the grass.

Of dark complexion and with unprocessed, thick unruly hair, Gloria towered over a diminutive Kenneth in whose features hard life had drawn crow's feet at the corners of his eyes and placed deep welts around his mouth. The darkness under his eyes bore testament to his past and present struggles. Her dark brown eyes greatly contrasted with his gray ones, which shone like a full moon whose reflection bounced off dark waters. Gloria, Kenneth's ventriloquist, made him feel like a visitor in his own life, as she controlled everything, except their three children. Quite the unconventional mother, her maternal instincts took flight with the birth of her first child and never returned, though she bore two more. But Kenneth had grown chummy with how unorthodox she was, and though she did not reply, he knew ultimately she would have the final say in his desire to work.

2. Tom McEnuff's Farm

Day turned to night and then started afresh. The sun yawned whilst stretching over the hills affirming its presence in Macca Tree. Kenneth rose early, escaped from the bed and the woman in it, scraped together his last ounce of courage and began his march to see Mr McEnuff.

Transported through the automatic gate by awe, Kenneth succumbed to the moment, skipping between yellow tractors with huge wheels stuck in red mud, an unlit cigarette hanging from the right side of his mouth. The view from outside the gates could not compare to the vision from within. The house was perched on a rising, near to Sweet River which ran throughout Macca Tree and the adjoining communities. The sweet citrusy smell of the orange trees, the roosters crowing announcing his arrival, the freshly ploughed earthy aroma of the fields and the distant calls of early birds broke the morning hush.

Being an early riser, Mr McEnuff was already tending to his squealing pigs at the foot of the incline when Kenneth walked up to him, head hung, shoulders shrugged and voice a little more than a whisper.

"You have a fine property Mr McEnuff. I hope one day I can afford something just like it." He was shy and dry in his approach.

"Being a hard worker has its perks, Kenneth. If a man is willing to put in hours nonstop before he breaks for coffee, then when he takes that break, he deserves it." Mr McEnuff smiled flashing even white teeth, confident in his profoundness. His five-foot-nine frame, clad in blue overalls and combat boots, and well-kept skin oozed years of prosperity.

"So what can I do for you?" his voice jolted Kenneth.

Hanging his inhibitions on a leash Kenneth replied, "I looking for work, Sar; anything at all."

Mr McEnuff affixed his gaze on Kenneth; he took in his well-patched, stained clothes then lifted his gaze to his eyes. Something about this little man stirred him. He said, "I could use some help in the sties starting today."

The suddenness of the employment shook Kenneth into a stammer. "That's...that's good for me. Lemme...lem... lemme just run home and tell Gloria."

He couldn't keep the stupid schoolboy grin off his face as he ran all the way home. When he came to his wire gate, he cleared it nimbly.

Gloria, who was still in her nightdress, emerged through the front door wiping her eyes. Kenneth's footsteps on the wooden verandah floor had awoken her from the sweet early-morning sleep.

"Is a chance for me to brush shoulder with the richest man in all Macca Tree, Top Road and Bottom Road. I intend to learn from him so I can teach Ken and Ron. I feel good about this Gloria!"

She was not amused. "Is that you wake me fa Kenneth? It normal for a man to work; I expect you to get a job. I not frighten for Mr McEnuff. Now, Frighten Friday, leave me mek me go back to sleep."

And just like that Kenneth was dismissed; a notch erased from his armour. He left for work with his tail between his legs.

Life in the sty among pitching flies and singing mosquitoes gave Kenneth purpose. Along with him, Foster, a forty-something farmer with worsening eyesight, two kids and bar debts to pay, set about cleaning the stench of the pigs. When Foster was not at the McEnuff's or in a bar, he was at home with his common-law wife, Ms Joyce and their two sons.

The sun had tightened its grip on Macca Tree that day and Kenneth and Foster took an unscheduled break fearing a heatstroke. Having fed the pigs a mixture of kitchen cuttings, grass and cane, both men sat wiping their brows with the back of their hands.

"Careful Kenneth," Foster warned, as the other man tried to pet one of the pigs. Since working at the McEnuff's, he was the closest thing Kenneth had to a friend. It was a pity that Gloria and Joyce could not find any points of agreement, Kenneth thought to himself.

"I hate this life Kenneth; I only want enough money to pay off mi debts and then I quit." Foster's words were heavy under his breath. Kenneth did not reply.

Silence enveloped the men.

"Well, I intend to buy a bicycle with my pay," Kenneth mumbled minutes later. "I just want to climb on to that bicycle and ride. When I was a boy I had one and it was fun. I want to feel like that again – free. I remember the wind and how mi clothes used to suck on to mi body as mi go down the hills. Mi heart used to race at the speed, but mi did love it, Foster. When I used to go round corners, you see mi head first and then the rest a mi body, and yuh better watch out when mi a come. So mi speed up, a so mi slow down; dem used to call me Dilly-Dally, yuh know Foster."

Mr McEnuff, clearing his throat, interrupted Kenneth's reveries, imposing on his prized memory.

"Oh, I never see you, Sar; we getting back to work now."

"That's OK, Kenneth," he said. "You can rest. It's terribly hot out here man."

Being painfully shy, Kenneth smiled and sat.

"Tiger and Cheddy going to join you boys today."

"Nice to make your acquaintances Sars," Kenneth said to the two much younger men. Foster staggered over and shook their hands. With hats pulled down to their noses, the faces of Tiger and Cheddy were unrecognizable, but their hands shook firm; Tiger's more so than Cheddy's. With scrutinizing gazes, they mapped out the two older men. In unison, Tiger and Cheddy returned to Mr McEnuff's voice. Pushing back his straw hat, exposing his handsome face, he concluded, "Unoo show them what to do." He then strode off adjusting the grass straw that always seem to have a place between his teeth.

3. State of Affairs

Friday came as if it followed behind Monday. Pay day, and Kenneth could not wait to open the small brown envelope. With his first salary, Kenneth bought a brand-new black BMX bicycle, hoping to make an impression on Gloria and Macca Tree.

The trip to purchase the bicycle took him to Savanna-la-Mar, the parish capital. Kenneth, Gloria and the children made the journey, huddled in a route taxi along with other residents. Overloaded and creaking from the weight, the taxicab journeyed around bends and across bridges into the bustling capital.

Kenneth wasted no time, while Gloria and Tamar moved to purchase some much-needed groceries for the house. Kenneth and the boys found a bicycle shop and chose the cheapest, shiny BMX that was their pride and joy. Gloria and the boys met back at the taxi stand for the trip back home, but Kenneth decided to spare himself the taxi fare by riding his new bicycle on the return journey.

Back at home, the bicycle was the only thing in the Manns' yard that promised new and different. It was placed proudly on the verandah like an ornament and a symbol of promised prosperity.

Soon Kenneth made a hobby of riding through the three communities with Gloria in tow. Passing each gate, perched on the handle bar, she cut her eyes in anticipation of the glares, humming her favourite hymn: *"What a frien we have in Jesus...hmmmmm...hmmm."*

It was on one of these outings and amidst issuing her routine cut-eyes she said,

"Kenneth, you goin' to have to stop working at the big yaad. You spending too much time at the McEnuffs."

"But Gloria, Foster and…"

"Don't 'but' me, Kenneth; I know what best for you. I don't want you working like a farmer horse. McEnuff have horse already. Is things like this mek Macca Tree don't respect wi. Why yu working for him? Why you don't start yuh own farm?"

"I learning how to mek a farm, Gloria," he replied, shifting on the bicycle seat.

"Well the lesson over. Yuh not going back to work there."

And that was that. Never one without a plan, Gloria spoke again, "I have a better idea in mind. I going to start a big money business in Macca Tree. Di people dem round here have money. Yuh see dem house? Not to mention di one McEnuff. Him is a millionaire businessman. I gwine to convince him to donate a small part of him great fortune to mi plan."

"So Gloria, in other words, all of a sudden you want something from him but I cyaa work for him?"

"Kenneth, you a try learn something from the devil was a bwoy and all now me a wait fi yuh stand up and be a man, but yuh is more like a sleeping dog."

"Gloria, why you must do me so? Gloria, I don't disrespect yuh, yuh nuh."

"The truth hurts Kenneth. Yuh too thin skin. Smaddy like yuh who can't stand di heat fi always stay outta my fire cause mi will burn yuh up."

Kenneth looked up at his woman, the mother of his children, his bride, and swallowed the boiling bile that had escaped from the pit of his stomach.

"Well, Kenneth, a so yuh meet me, a so mi a go stay. A washover ring pon mi finger nah go change that."

Gloria read his thoughts.

Vexed and defeated, Kenneth rode on like a bullied schoolboy with a crippling need for abuse. Returning home a little after seven that night, they were greeted by their teary eyed, running nosed, hungry-mouthed trio. Emerging from the darkness of abandonment, they challenged each other for Kenneth and Gloria's attention.

In another community and under different circumstances, residents would have posted posters, ransacked buildings, kicked down doors, and walked the streets until the wee hours, being sick with worry that the parents of three children were missing. But this was Macca Tree and these were the Manns. So in this real and unforgiving world, the community members would themselves banish Gloria and Kenneth faster than the speed of lightening. These forgotten children, with their tear-stained faces, sucked their swelling thumbs by the roadside, looking for the kindness of any stranger. Next to the dogs, they were the most popular on the sidewalk, day or night. Notorious throughout Macca Tree and with the odds stacked high against them, they could not keep out of trouble.

Immune to her children's need for affection and to what anyone thought of that, cold-as-steel Gloria stepped past them in a hurry to pick up a black book with her jottings. Kenneth draped an arm around each boy, who hung to it like a life source. Tamar, with one hand, tagged behind Gloria, hanging on to her flowing skirt.

Like her mother, Tamar's thick unruly hair was unkempt and sticking out in all directions. The stuffed animal in her free hand had a checkered past and could have been a dust rag, as it was a ready dirt magnet. Being seven years-old, she was the baby of the bunch and one year younger than her brother, Ron, who was hopeless at being a child. Clinging to his father with one hand, he held a bat in his other hand. Even though Ron could barely hit a ball, he loved playing with his homemade bat and juice-box ball. Many times his missed judgment sent the ball flying, ripped speed, through the neighbour's patterned glass windows. The smashing of these windows was compounded by the fact that they were never replaced by Kenneth or Gloria. For this, the family was known by all as 'The curse of Macca Tree', a name coined by their neighbour, Ms Dolly.

They entered Gloria's room after her and Kenneth. The couple had moved into separate bedrooms following the episode with Kenneth disturbing her rest to relay news of his new-found job at Mr McEnuff's.

Stretching under her flat floral pillow, Gloria reached for her black book. Opening the pages, she displayed leaves with pencil drawings of residents. A name was affixed to each stick figure, with an amount of money befitting in hard numbers. The drawings were on top of each other with each figure getting closer towards the top of the page; at the very top was the name McEnuff.

"Look at this Kenneth, I already maths out how this thing going to work."

Kenneth sat next to her and pulled the smoke out of a cigarette, trapping the children in the exhaled smog.

"What that Gloria?"

"Mi figet yu can't read. Well, I going to ask people to invest some money wid mi, like a pardna and give dem back some money monthly. The more money yuh have is the more yuh expected to get back. Is interest dem call it. The more people that invest, the more money yuh get monthly."

"Di people round here don't like wi Gloria, how yuh gonna mek dem do it?"

"Don't worry 'bout that; all will be revealed in time. Is me dem don't like Kenneth. Dem don't have any problem wid yuh."

With a wave of his hand and a squirm on his face, Kenneth walked off to his room with Ken Jr and Ron, leaving Gloria to her tactics and a sleeping Tamar at her feet.

4. Pastor's Wife and the Plan

Two weeks crammed into one day. The sun and rain took turns pelting Macca Tree and the surrounding communities like an angry hammer; first the rolling thunder then the lightening whipping the skies as if warning the Manns to leave Macca Tree, but defiant Gloria just looked up, cut her eyes and sang: "*What a frien we have in Jesus....*"

It was as if the elements gave up, being no match for her. The sun appeared to have done its best to burn out her demons, but Gloria befriended her iron tub; though too small for her to fit in, Gloria forced herself into the pan full of cool river water and sat in it with her legs hanging over its edges. The hairy mango tree which hovered over her bled in places where her children had chopped it as if preparing for a challenge with Paul Bunion.

Under the tree is where she sat, duly scrubbed and splashed with Khus Khus she had purchased in Savanna-la-Mar, when Pastor's wife stopped by to see her. It was no surprise to anyone, as Monica may have been fulfilling her godly duty by trying to convert Gloria.

Walking through Macca Tree, Monica looked as though she could have been her husband's daughter. With a smile, she kidnapped the reasoning of teenage boys like Ms Joyce's sons and made them run to church. With a swing of her skirt she made men like Foster not want to marry the likes of Ms Joyce, but rather re-experience their youth just so they would have a chance with her. Bouncing her buttocks up and down in the spirit anywhere and anytime was her favourite pastime, and with the high splits and low cuts that she wore, there was little left to the imagination.

A paragon of virtue, Monica daintily opened the wire gate leading to the Manns and greeted Gloria outside the house.

Escorted to the veranda, Monica's concern stained her face though she tried to hide the scorn with each carefully placed step. The vast contrasts of both women were overwhelming, but what stood out the most was the rebel in Gloria versus the polished pastor's wife. The children came out of nowhere and in the frightful moment circled and ogled the attractive newcomer, who quickly dodged their prying eyes, moving closer to Gloria, with her high heels striking a rhythm on the ground, her actions likening to a rebuke.

The children reeked of wet dog, having just given their mangy mongrel a bath. At her shunning, Ken Jr went back to tormenting the ackee tree by scratching their surname into its trunk with a sharpened blade. Known by all as Ken, he was the spitting image of his father. He exited the womb fighting for survival, so it wasn't hard for him to readily assume the responsibility of his brother and sister early on; it was he who had patched the broken floors of their house with stones, giving new meaning to hardwood floor and tough love. It was extremely hard being the firstborn of Gloria and Kenneth, with no manly figure to guide him. His mother being the devil made him the devil's spawn and a ready nuisance in Macca Tree.

Monica was well aware of the stigma and stood at the threshold between the veranda and living room for almost five minutes, marvelling at the potholes in the floor and searching for a solid place to step inside. Finally, she tiptoed to the table in the middle of an empty dust-filled dining room and took a seat on a three-foot chair, the fourth replaced by a block. She looked around at the dilapidated structure, surmising that it was not fit to be inhabited by even animals. But being used to the degradation, Gloria just continued about her business. She had put a pot of water on the already lit coal stove and reached for a plastic bag of cornmeal that perched on a greasy shelf above it. Kenneth had forgotten to pick up his half flask of white rum when he left home that morning. Gloria lifted the bottle from its seat on the dusty wooden table and tilted it to examine its content. She took up a glass that Ken had washed earlier and poured the draining of liquor from the bottle, then handed the glass to Monica.

It took six sips of Kenneth's white rum for Monica to accept that she was in the midst of the menacing Manns' mansion. Looking at the back of the house to where Gloria was, she saw the sink full of last night's pots and pans. The ticking clock became loud with each gulp of the liquor she downed.

Monica's visit to the Manns did not escape the residents of Macca Tree. Ms Joyce and a few other women took up positions in their front yards to get a piece of the expected action. The stares from the women embarrassed Monica into declaring her purpose.

"Is a little prayer meeting wi having, Ms Joyce," she shouted; her hip-hugging silk dress twisted and rode her bulky frame as if in tandem with her words.

"Prayer meeting? That yard and everything in it beyond prayer," Ms Joyce shouted back. "Just holler if yuh need help," she shouted from her vantage point.

"Eek!" A startled Monica brushed a wave of chi-chi dust falling from the roof, unpleasantly powdering her well made-up face, smudging her blush in the process.

"See it deh, demons on the attack!" Joyce shouted. But Monica showed she could handle herself, declaring the presence of God and exploiting her agility with unknown tongues. Her tongue swung into action like a pendulum as she gave in to the language of the Spirit.

"In the name of Jesus! I declare that the demons of hell will not prevail in this place! Oooh, makashamca...ohh, Lamb of God, rise up in this place. Yosholoka...!"

Gloria hummed in reverence, as her mind raced to capture the full confidence of Monica who was a gift to her fast-developing big money scheme.

As Monica shook with the Holy Spirit, Gloria's mind danced with anticipation as her plan took shape.

Once done with the charade, Gloria, ready, putting on her most pious game face, took Monica's hand.

"Ms Monica, while you were praying, the Lord spoke to me. He gave me a plan that will raise money for the church and for our community. He said, Gloria! I have chosen you to bless Macca Tree. You shall be a blessing and all shall come to you and be blessed. Hallelujah!"

Monica's eyes opened wide as she listened eagerly. The church was in urgent need of funds and God can use anything, so Pastor had said, to bless His people. Gloria was certainly anything.

Monica looked keenly at Gloria, and she could feel the Spirit coming on again.

"Hallelujah! God has sent you Gloria to rescue His people!"

Joyce and the other women had entered the Mann's yard almost involuntarily as Monica continued her declaration over Gloria, who was now fully prostrate on the dirty wooden floor wriggling for dear life.

"Run go fi Pastor! Run," Ms Joyce bellowed.

"No need to call Pastor, I can handle this!" Monica calmed the growing crowd.

Gloria steadied her body and edged into the sitting position.

"Can you rise to your feet, prophetess?" Monica asked. In one fell swoop Gloria, the condemned, had become the consecrated.

Her plan to use Kenneth to woo the confidence of Macca Tree was now null and void. Monica was to be her saviour.

5. The More Things Change...

When Kenneth told Foster about the latest Gloria-sanctioned act against him, he did not know it would spread like wildfire, nor was he prepared for the backlash she would receive. On a midmorning Saturday, while the sun bronzed the earth and the animals chimed in a cacophony ushering Kenneth along the spine of Macca Tree looking like an old shirt hung from a nail, he encountered Joyce with her pudding pan on her head, full of freshly cut callaloo ready for sale. Before his morning greeting escaped his lips, she shut him up with her attack.

"I wud ask how yuh look so, but Foster tell mi. No baba, but yuh is a puppet, she a pull all yuh strings!" Joyce told Kenneth.

"Mi love har, Joyce. But she a drive mi crazy. I feel black and blue," Kenneth replied.

"Well, yuh love white rum too, and that nuh good fi yuh either. I don't even know what yuh find attractive about Gloria, that woman not even ugly; she have nutten fi do wid looks...but I guess every hoe have dem stick a bush."

"Joyce, is mi wife yuh talking bout.Yuh best kibba yuh mouth...before she hear yuh."

Gloria's leash on Kenneth provoked not only Joyce but the foundation of Macca Tree. Their sophomoric antics and casual bicycle journeys through the communities raised the suspicions of Top and Bottoms road residents alike.

"Dem looking something fi teef," was the common cry. But still the two travelled, watching boys catch crabs in the swampy water along Bottom Road or stopping by pastures to observe animals grazing on the lush greenness of Top Road. Gloria tickled the residents with the way she conveniently hung up her cape of motherhood to bask daily in the golden evening sun. Enjoying the breeze as she hummed along, she ignored the curse words that flew from the lips of her children as they played in the open yard.

Monica accepting her proposal was a catalyst to Gloria's new bouts of joy as she balanced on the handlebar with her newly consecrated hands in the prayer position for all and sundry to see. On one of their evening journeys, Kenneth stopped for her to buy a sandwich of spiced bun and cheese at Maas Joscelyn's shop. She sank her teeth into the soft brown bun, stuffed with the bright yellow cheese as she settled under the little bus shed at the front of Top Road community. This was Gloria's stress-relief corner and her escape spot from the terrors she called children. Many times in the height of her discontent, Kenneth found her there just sitting, thinking. The bun was a little past its sell-by date, she thought, but the idea of setting up the scheme was so good that she wouldn't even attack Maas Joscelyn. She ate it in mouthfuls, enjoying the moment while feeding the hard crusts to the lingering mongrels.

"Kenneth, I think the plan gwine work, yuh know. I have the perfect partner."

Kenneth just sat on the bar of the parked bicycle and stared at his wife gorging down the brown sandwich. In times like this, Kenneth remembered why he had married Gloria too many years ago; she had dreams and made him believe, even for a fleeting moment, that he could do anything.

"Gloria, I hope is not a hurry-come-up-scheme yuh know. I can't relocate again. The children need to settle down and go school. I want some respect round here and I don't think that if this don't work out Macca Tree going to keep us here or tek us back if we run away again."

But Gloria was bursting at the seams, bleeding joy and possibilities.

"Kenneth, when this work out you can lay brick and maata and mek a pigsty fi yuhself. Yuh can plant yuh cane just like Mr McEnuff."

Kenneth smiled at the idea of having esteem in Macca Tree and starting a trade for his sons. In the moment, he did not feel as though Gloria's soul lies only at the bottom of her feet and was spelt a different way. He didn't even care about what people thought of her. He just listened to Bob Marley's 'No Woman nuh Cry' playing on the radio from Maas Joscelyn shop, soaked up the evening sun and tasted the air that smelt of cooling cornmeal pudding that would be on Mary's pastry shelf tomorrow.

"Yuh in a good mood, Glor," he admired. "The last time I see yuh this happy was years ago when the partner plan was in full swing. Yuh know I spent years searching for that missing spec of joy in yuh?"

And now that Kenneth found it, he wanted to capitalize; he wanted to share this with his children; he wanted to savour its sweetness forever.

"Memba di kids, Glor. We have to go now. Yuh going to cook tonight? I so hungry I feel I cudda eat a cow and use the calf wipe mi mouth."

She laughed at his eagerness as she swallowed the last of the bun and cheese sandwich.

As if in deep contemplation, she spoke again, "Yuh know I will be a good mother when I rich, right Kenneth?"

Without thinking he blurted out, "I really hope so."

His words fell on her hard like the rock of Gibraltar slipping from its base.

"This is why I don't get soft yuh know, Kenneth, because yuh always disturb the moment. I just need yuh support, I want to know yuh believe in mi."

Kenneth threw up his hands and shook his head.

"Just carry mi home!" she commanded. And there it was again, the devil in Gloria had arisen once more. The ride home was less pleasant. Going over the steep hills, Kenneth's breath came too frequently and too deeply. The weight of the world was indeed on his shoulders, competing with Gloria's ample anatomy firmly secured on the handlebar. His pounding heart punctuated each of Gloria's sighs whilst she complained about his slow pace over the hills.

Kenneth knew this was his punishment for having challenged her efforts as a mother. But, that he could bear; he had no immediate regret for his little sprig of boldness.

By the time they got home, the place resembled Gloria's mood. Ken Jr, Ron and Tamar felt the blunt of her anger. She shouted them out of her way and chose her black book over their advances.

Sprawled on her belly, Gloria studied her etched sketches while the four members of her family, standing at her doorway, stared at her back and bobbing head as though their future was projected there.

The day ended as it started, shadowy and undiagnosed, with Gloria locked away in the arms of her new dreams. The children struggled to swallow the overcooked chicken back Kenneth prepared for them that night.

"Thanks Daddy, wi know yuh trying," Ken Jr said.

Retiring to bed, all four closed their eyes to another meaningless memory.

6. Seeding the Deal

In the following days, for two reasons much was expected of Kenneth's older brother and well-known farmer in Macca Tree, Darcy, with whom Kenneth did not speak. Kenneth, who had become a vagabond roaming the community, began worrying about the actions of his son, Ken. Residents reported that things were going missing in areas the child frequented. But it was Darcy's wife, Dolly, a 45-year-old born-again believer, who openly displayed her disgust for her in-laws at every chance and vehemently insisted in her high-pitched voice that they return to Trelawny, where Kenneth was born.

With overdyed silver-hair-turned-blue, Dolly was the village doctor who knew everything and had something to say about it.

But Gloria, who by now had won the confidence of the over-churched in Macca Tree, was now referred to as 'Prophetess' by those who dared not crossed God. Sporting plaid headwraps with two pencils ready to take notes, she remained soberly uncaring and did as she so pleased, disregarding the complaints about her son.

"Di whole a unu a liad. Mi pickney nuh need fi teef. Anybody come to mi wid such chat again, mark mi words, mi a go fix yuh business fi yuh. I will take yuh name to the throne myself! All you Dolly, wid yuh head looking like a fowl roost, mind yuh mouth. Yuh can't talk against the prophet of God any which way yuh want!"

Still, Dolly preached: "I don't get why you can't care for your kids, Kenneth. I not talking to the heathen Gloria, but I think you have more heart and will listen to reason. Dem too young to be on dem own, and Ken is a little teef."

To this he replied in a moronic tone, "Ms Dolly, Gloria change, yuh know."

But having her way meant Gloria was a god. Bent on starting her plan, she followed up Monica. This time they chose the cool of night to meet. Being at the end of the road, there was no street light to illuminate the meeting at the Manns' mansion.

Prophetess Gloria divulged the sacred plot within the empty weightily webbed walls. Thoughts of money moved Monica mightily. And being a past partner in crime with school-aged Gloria did much to quickly seal the new bond. Sneaking into Macca Tree from Top Road was hard for her because anyone could recognize that buxom body.

Monica wore a black hoodie and sneakers that night, passing only Tiger and Cheddy on the road, ignoring the sounds they were making as though they were losing air. "Pssst."

Finally, she made it to Gloria's. Cutting to the chase, Monica spoke quickly.

"So what yuh sey yuh want mi to do Gloria?" the pastor's wife straightened in her seat. "Tell me everything from scratch."

"I have an idea for di church that God relay to mi in a dream. It will get the whole community rich quick and with a rich congregation, yuh will have a rich church. But even though is my idea, I want you to head it. Macca Tree stomach you, dem respect yuh, yuh is the pastor's wife. Di plan pretty simple."

Gloria reached for her book. "First thing, get the Macca Tree, Top and Bottom road people dem to invest $5,000 each in a church scheme and dem will get interest every month. Call it a church building fund."

She explained that the first to invest will get back what they put in plus interest after two months, but they can only get their money back if they get two other persons to invest.

"So by the end of the first two months, we will have enough investors to pay the first set of people and since everybody bringing in others we will always have money!"

"This is genius!" Monica exclaimed. "A truly God tell you dis! We will call it planting a seed!"

"Yes! A so we must call it! Thank you Lord!" Gloria shouted.

Silence suddenly engulfed Monica. Gloria stared at her in anticipation of her words.

"Why yuh think anybody would invest wid wi? We is not a bank. Yuh asking mi to play wid God money Gloria."

Gloria was quick to the draw.

"Yuh going give Him back every penny. It will be a good venture for the church; just think bout it. Start it small and gradually include more people so the interest will flow. Next thing yuh know di whole a Westmoreland inna it. Think bout the money the church wudda mek. Yuh cudda put on a whole heap a crusade, enlarge the church...buy a new car?"

"Yuh sure it will work? I don't want to get in trouble yuh know." Monica mumbled.

"It will work because every mickle mek a muckle. Just introduce it in church on Sunday. Dolly won't suspect anything if yuh mek it look like a church initiative. She a di treasurer; she love money too."

"Memba wha happen last time when yu run 'way wid di people dem partner money, Gloria? Trouble nuh set like rain yuh know Gloria."

"Ay, ay, ay. Yu still deh pon dat? What yu did do wid your share? Remember a nuh mi one did benefit?"

"Alright, alright; mi ask forgiveness a long time ago and I hardly wear the frock mi did buy out of it. I just concerned. Whey Kenneth? Him know about dis?"

"Well him know I have a plan. Him a lose him head since I fired him from working for Mr McEnuff."

Unleashing her deadly charm, Gloria continued: "Yuh look good deh though for smaddy whose age drop off calendar."

"Thanks for di complement, cousin." Monica smiled then continued again, "So is where you get the idea?"

"A man named Karl Hilton has a big one like it in town and it doing really well. Now is a good time to pitch the product, so wi can show people sey it work."

"So is not God give yuh di vision? You is a ginal yuh know, Gloria." Monica giggled. "Yuh can't tell anybody that though."

Monica proffered her commitment. "I will do it; sounds like a good plan, and I never refuse money."

Gloria's relief erupted into a belly laugh. "Well you have a sugar daddy posing as a pastor and robbing the church money to prove dat!" she giggled.

"Ridicule not the Lord's anointed Gloria. If yuh gwine make fun of mi husband, mi might just change mi mind."

"Alright then. But nuh breathe a word yet sey mi a part a it. Introduce it without calling mi name to the church. I don't want people fi get antsy. Mi is a silent partner at the beginning, but mi will run things behind the scene," Gloria cautioned. "Dem neva call yuh pretty dunce fi nutten."

No need to argue with Gloria, Monica wrapped things up. Stepping back into the moonlight, she felt God retreating from her heart, her soul and her life; a feeling she had become accustomed to. There was no one outside to witness a godly conversion, no Gloria praising God on the top of her voice and no need for Monica to speak in tongues, flash holy water or read a Psalm. She simply disappeared down the asphalt; her impending utopia was her only company as she departed.

7. The Emasculation of Kenneth and the Rise of Ken

With Monica as her prime partner again, Gloria had no need for Kenneth. The scheme was taking shape beautifully.

Kenneth's behaviour started to mirror the weirdly patterned shirts he wore, and like his thick overgrown moustache, joblessness and the bicycle no longer shining and laid up most days, he faded into purposelessness.

In two dreary months, Kenneth was to become Macca Tree's drunk and when clear-headed, his low, weak, slow voice could not break through the veil of silence that had engulfed him. Kenneth removed himself from positive possibilities and was relegated to being Gloria's bicycle chauffeur, the few times when he got the wheels to work.

One fateful night as he tried to make his way home defying his drunken stupor, a group of boys from Bottom Road rid him of the jalopy that he once called a bicycle. A herd of stray dogs approached him. Assuming that the lump that a fallen Kenneth had become in the middle of the clean-swept street was a feast, they sniffed, claimed with their urine, and then, like Gloria, rejected him.

With Kenneth reduced to nothing and Gloria needing a new toy to distract her until the money started to roll in from her plan, she capitalized on the attention from the only person in the community that favoured her – old, overworked shopkeeper Joscelyn. Gloria's tainted past was no stranger to Joscelyn, and her company provided him sweet comfort in his loneliness.

Joscelyn owned a yellow four-bedroom house that was hidden behind flower gardens, shrubs and trees and buried in silence; that's until Gloria became his tail and trailed him home. He was a man in his late fifties who spoke with a stutter. His thick-framed glasses did not give him vision any more than his oversized clothes made him muscular. His second skin of waterboots had more endurance than he did, but Gloria ignored his faint manhood because it was bested only by his money.

He carried a staunch defence of his new-found girlfriend.

"...She goo..ooo...oood enough ffffff...for me." This was his standard ender to every Gloria-laced conversation.

Like an animal defending its young, he did not even want breeze to blow on Gloria. His ferocity knew no bounds and he even developed distaste for her children, blaming them for the negative image of Gloria in Macca Tree. He especially did not like Ken.

"Him too dry yeye and barefaced, Gloria," he said of the boy.

Ken Jr had stolen his goat, and his lasting impression of the child could not be diminished by his love for his mother.

Joscelyn's hatred of Ken reverberated throughout Top Road, Bottom Road and Macca Tree. But despite this, the boy held a steadfast love for all three places deep down in his gut. He enjoyed the clean street and found the orchard-like existence irresistible. He loved that there were narrow lanes leading to each house from the road and that the properties were like a world unto themselves. He loved how Mr McEnuff's house was a focal point and sat on the hillside as a landmark overseeing the other houses.

He was especially obsessed with the aroma of food on fire that constantly hung in the air and the strange way the residents took pride in their community. But most of all, he had grown fond of the rum bars where he spent most of his time; hanging with the older men, he drank beer from squat dark-brown bottles and sometimes enjoyed the tangy fare in a green one.

Ken once attempted the famous John Crow Batty rum which he heard was made from the cane harvested from the McEnuff's field. Not one to pass on a bet, he downed a cupful of the substance while holding his nose. Among those applauding that effort was his father, Kenneth, who treated him as though he was an old friend.

"Unu pay mi bwoy," Kenneth stammered as Ken claimed the $2,000 prize from the pot of trumped-up money, saved for whoever could drink the prohibited tonic in less than 30 seconds. Now a hall-of-famer at Joe's bar, Ken was able to use his gains to purchase food that night. Mapping his way around Macca Tree, Ken had indeed become a thorn in the flesh of many, one even more pointed than his mother.

8. Planting the Seed

Gloria and Monica had put the finishing touches on their plan and now it was time to roll it out. If one was not accustomed to the revival of the Macca Tree Born Again Church of the Apostles, one would think that the rapture was at hand.

This was another typical Sunday, with the exception that it was also the day of revelation for Monica. Macca Tree, Top Road and Bottom Road residents crammed into the brownstone walls, almost teeming out of the multicoloured windows which trembled with the vibration of stomping feet. The sounds of praise seemed to lift the roof from its hurricane straps. The choir wore blood-red, floor-length gowns signalling the importance of the service; from all indications, the battle was on for the remaining women to outdress each other. Their colourful houses faded in comparison to cheerful pieces they wore to church, complete with hats and high heels that restricted their movement, except when they were in the Spirit.

The men were more reserved, but always enjoyed the show the women put on, especially Monica. Not only was it a competition for best dressed but for the longest prayer, loudest singer and even who could contribute the most offering. Not to be outdone in any area, Monica prided herself on her many accomplishments; today as she sat on the pulpit next to her 60 year-old husband, looking down at the pew, her oversized hat conveniently hid her transgressions and shielded her from the stares she often enjoyed, but dreaded today.

Apart from her suddenly active conscience, Monica was very much aware of everything today because she was on the verge of planting a seed she hoped would grow into a towering tree. She was aware of the wind howling at the trees, the grass swaying in chorus to the conducting wind, the sun retreating behind dark clouds and even the silence of Sweet River gurgling alongside the church. It was the same river that had washed away her sins years ago when she decided to serve the Lord. Now it was offering her no solace as she looked on at the congregation partaking of the Lord's Supper.

As a young girl, Monica knew not to play around with that which represented the body and blood of Jesus Christ. She heard about people who had become sick because they were unclean and had eaten the bit of bread and drank the grape juice. Surely, she had trespassed in the path of unrighteousness before and was forgiven, but this that she was about to attempt was presumptuous.

Monica descended the stairs towards the two male ushers and set down her King James Version Bible wrapped in a gold holder; her knees buckled beneath her weighty thoughts. Knocking on God for reason, she prayed he would send her a sign if she was not to partake of the supper. But the prayer line was disconnected and she received no answer from heaven. Now standing at the altar, she felt in her Spirit that there was someone watching her from outside the room. Looking up she spotted Gloria; it was the last image she saw before passing out, bringing the feast to a standstill.

But within minutes Monica gathered her consciousness and had the full attention of everyone.

"Brethren, I didn't mean to scare yuh. But I was being disobedient and the Lord had to stop mi in my tracks. He has placed something in my heart for a while now, but it's time I shared it with you."

She was helped up to her feet by two of the apprehensive male ushers who were only too eager to touch her.

"Friends, for a while the Lord has been talking to me about the state of the congregation. Yes, wi drop off shape but He gave me a vision on how to take back wi rightful place as a church and as individuals. The Lord wants to supply all our needs according to His riches in glory."

"Amen, speak Lord," the eager congregation erupted. The women were now standing on their feet, rocking, awaiting the signal that Pentecost was on the verge of its second coming.

"Friends, God want you to help Him help you by planting a monetary seed. In my vision, as in Corinthians, He said every man should give what he has decided in his heart to give, not reluctantly or under compulsion, for He loves a cheerful giver."

"Oh fill her Lord!" The usual suspects shouted from their wobbly standing in the pews.

Now more than ever, Monica was in her element with all ears at her command. Convinced the Lord was using her as a vessel, picking up her Bible and hoisting it over her head, exposing well-manicured red nails, she continued to preach to the faithful.

"The Lord said, 'I will help My people help themselves because upon them I build My church... ah.' Friends, He wants you to put away a minimum of $5,000 each; from this, He instructed me to give you interest after two months... ah...and then monthly thereafter. It's so exclusive...ah, that only you present will benefit. But friends, He also says, that if you...ah, want to multiply your returns, you can invite others...ah, to share in this glorious occasion. But only if you want more, only if you want to increase your overflow."

The congregation exploded. Deafening decibels of hallelujah and babbling of unknown tongues drowned out rising chatter. Monica danced around on one foot, her behind jumping and jerking frantically, heavy with the eyes of the brethren. Observing the distraction brought on by the frenzied flock, Monica unleashed a barrage of unknown tongues; glancing over at the window, she got thumbs up from Gloria, grinning from ear to ear. But Dolly, whose eyes were too fast for her own good, was not amused. She muttered to herself, daring not to disturb the brethren in their moment of worship.

"So why you and not me Monica? I am the treasurer; why not give me the plan to build the church. I pray too and you is not more Christian than me," she said to herself.

Gloria, who had drawn near to Dolly did not miss the whispered remark.

"You questioning the Lord's messenger, Dolly? That's why him never tell you, you not a believer, oh ye of little faith!" Gloria smiled wickedly.

"Sister Dolly, I must say this sound like a blessing in disguise," Ms Joyce blurted as she looked for wisdom and approval in Dolly's eyes.

Murmurs gave way to her single, subdued voice.

"So Sister Monica, when the Lord say we must plant the seed and where?"

"The sooner the better Joyce; like I said, it rested with me for a while now. He said all of you must be on board for maximum result in the church and the community, so I took the liberty to go ahead and do some calculation for the entire membership...at His instruction of course. He directed me to watch over the funds, so take it to me." In a move to kill any doubt, she added while rocking herself, "Brethren, I feel a weight has been lifted now that I have delivered his words."

Monica reached into her bosom and pulled out a string purse. She opened it with eager fingers and pulled out a stack of $100 bills.

"See here, this is my contribution to the seed, this is my seed money. I am planting the first seed!"

The church erupted in hallelujahs once more.

"Well, I like it and we wouldn't want to displease the Lord now, would we saints?" Joyce declared.

They agreed, to the amazement of Monica and the pleasure of Gloria.

"Well, brothers and sisters, seeing you allowing God to have His way, we will have a special prayer meeting tonight. Come out with your funds so Pastor and I can bless it. The Lord doesn't want us to linger as He has a huge blessing in store for us."

"Hallelujah, glory!" The congregation launched into a medley of hymns and choruses. The organist led the worship by fingering the keys that tuned in the old favourite and the congregation sang out the words which they all seemed to know by heart.

"What a friend we have in Jesus..."

Outside, Gloria tiptoed to the back of the church, exiting the same way she had entered. She could not have done it better herself.

9. No Glory for Gloria

It had been one week since the plan saw its spirited birth. Alive with hope, the residents paraded to each other's house speaking of the amount they each invested and how much they stood to gain.

"Well, I clean out my mattress yuh know Dolly," Joyce said as she sipped a cup of search-mi-heart tea, leaning over the fence that separated them.

'I was iffy at first too, but I put mi little together."

Distracted by Gloria who walked past them without even a sideward glance, Joyce continued,

"If only wi could get she outta Macca Tree. For her alone, this place would not have received such a blessing."

These two women did not buy into Gloria's role as a prophetess; hissing their teeth in choral precision, they returned to discussing the God plan. Hope was in the air and the smell of everything else paled in comparison to that of the promised pending prosperity. Such a blessing was in store that even the houses in Macca Tree shone brightly without a fresh coat of paint and the fruit trees bore out of season. The mangy dogs were fed because there was expectation of excess everywhere and all was topped off with a new crusade to give God thanks for his mysterious ways.

Always a target, the Manns continued to be the subject of Macca Tree bickering and nonstop prayers from the church members who constantly prayed for their exorcism from demonic possession. The unscheduled prayer meetings at their gate gave Monica a reason to roll out her tongues for the building of faith. But the wasted words and prayers were just that, wasted. The family continued unsaved and unabashed despite the dashing of holy water and the bamboo cross placed at their gateway.

Prophetess Gloria joined the chanting women during one of the meetings at her gate and added a thorny crown she wove from a whimpy branch she broke from the macca tree in her yard. When the women departed, Ken removed the cross and used the wood to make fuel for the Manns' fire.

Monica was mindful of her strained allegiance to Gloria as she was seen as leader of the female prayer assault at the wire gate, so she soon made her way to the ramshackle house to make amends.

"You know I have to keep up appearances, right Gloria? Don't take it personal when I lead the church to your gate. It's all a part of the bigger plan."

"Just don't forget is who in charge here, Monica," Gloria answered.

As the investments rolled in, Macca Tree rocked with rumours. Some were quoting millions, others multimillions in dollars and expectation.

"The news already spreading, but wi have to maintain control. After one month, wi tek the second round. We have to play it smart to sustain the plan."

"I like this chemistry between us Gloria; yuh making me dare to believe in second chances. But I must trust you Gloria; don't take the money this time."

"Yuh know I had to tek di partner money, Monica, mama needed surgery. Was I to make har dead without trying?"

"She dead anyway; better yuh did put di money to better use."

"Like you who buy clothes? Well I learn my lesson; I not caring about no one like that again. Love only hurt yuh heart and yuh head." She paused, then continued again fixatedly. "Monica, I want a fully furnished house in Macca Tree. Compared to the old house, this one will be a step up from broken door knobs and worn-out springless couch. Mi want leather sofa and pretty cushions with flowers pattern. Mi want wooden shutters and vases of all shapes and sizes like the McEnuffs. Mi want big antique furniture, and lace curtains too."

"All in time Gloria, all in time; just stick to the plan come what may. So yuh don't think a bank safer to keep di money, mek it gwaan earn interest?"

"That's the beauty of it; people will think it in a bank and nuh look fi it here. Plus I expect this thing to get big, so I can't carry it to a bank; we will have to declare where wi get so much money. And whose name we would put di account in anyway? Too much complications, mek it stay here."

That was that.

In the days that followed, Gloria gave all her attention to her brainchild whilst continuing to ignore her children and husband, unaffected by the gossip. The unrequited love that suffered Kenneth to wrath on most days was soothed, often enough by rum consumption, for him to do nothing about Gloria's open affair with Joscelyn. Many times, she awoke with the rooster's crow in the wee hours of the morning and floated home from Joscelyn's yellow house, riding the waves of stares from the sea of shocked neighbours peeping through Macca Tree's colourful curtains.

10. Ken Feels the Heat

Since her return to the community, this was the first time Gloria was consistently happy, and Kenneth, being a little more than a moving log, was not about to spoil her joy.

Another two weeks passed and the rave mounted from just persons lining up to get on board. For Gloria this signalled a coming to terms with the reality that by embracing her plan, Macca Tree had indirectly embraced her. She hated being on the outside but was determined to be a success and accomplish her dreams even if it meant being a ghost. The success of this plan was not something she wanted just a little bit – Gloria needed it to work so she could stop living vicariously through Monica. The first set of seeds had already borne fruit and the majority of the investors had taken the bait to roll over their investment for a second time. The few who asked for their seed with the promised interest were paid promptly. There was a steady flow of seeds and Monica was reporting a healthy state of the funds. She had made a small contribution to the church of $10,000 and Pastor had welcomed the money and prayed over it. Monica's handling of the funds did not bother her husband, who also gave her full control of all that he possessed.

Standing at her gate, Gloria watched as the Macca Tree residents returned from the church crusades with their noses turned up against her.

At the same time, Ken stepped out of the yard and on to the street with no shirt, clad only in old cut-off khaki pants, unbuttoned but zipped. All the remnants of the long hot summer had blazed past October and November and retreated on that cold Tuesday afternoon in early December.

Turning to Gloria he said, "Mi a guh fi Daddy; mi hear him on the sidewalk again."

With no friends or school to attend, Ken had got accustomed to wandering the street, though he was treated worse than a scorned leper. But, like a boomerang, he always bounced back in true Ken style, much to the horror of everyone. Watching him walk down the street, Gloria saw that Ken's young feet told an old tale; the cracks were evidence of constant shoelessness. Unsure of the emotion she felt, she said: "You making a name for yuhself as a send-out-boy in Macca Tree. Stop it; dem not better than yuh. And just go get Kenneth; don't stay out beyond midnight."

With her plan in motion, Gloria began to feel sudden surges of motherhood. But the damage was already done to the lawless brood she bore. Ken, the now notorious thief, had many scars to show for it; as often as he was caught he was wounded. There were chops to his head, scratches to his arms and even burns to his back. Of slim build, ten-year-old Ken was about four feet two inches with uncut hair and a chipped front tooth which was a souvenir from one of his many escapades. With light-brown eyes and a straight nose, Ken could have been handsome and probably still could be with some care. As on that day, he was often the one called to pick up Kenneth from the wayside or a bar, when he passed out. Never complaining, it became part of his daily routine to see his father's dazed face and smell sour vomit on his breath when he protested as Ken carried him home, bearing the weight of past regrets.

Never one to take her eyes off the prize, Gloria did not see Kenneth transcending into a lonely middle-aged caveman. It was Ken who witnessed daily his father's retreat into overwhelming despair, but was handicapped by his youth and knew not how to mediate.

The crisp air cut at Ken's bare back as he headed to the bar for his father; in his signature khaki cut-offs, he was unmistaken and some doors closed when his small feet were heard pattering down the somewhat sticky asphalt that was emitting the heat it had gobbled up while the sun was out. But Ken's feet only made noise when he wanted to because, at will, the thief in him was as silent as a waveless ocean.

Walking up the street, the sweet smell of fried chicken perfumed and provoked Ken as it emphasized his hunger, which gave him a call to action. The sweet oniony smell of steamed fish and fried chicken back from two of the shops along the road triggered his longing for a home-cooked meal. The idea to grab something to eat attached itself to him like the devil affixed to a shoulder whispering evil deeds. He walked past Ms Joyce's house, but backed up as he saw her pot perched on the wooden fire in her yard.

"Jackpot!" he grinned. Squatting in the hibiscus bush, he watched as 50-year-old Ms Joyce put the seasoned meat in her pot and returned to her chores inside. Ken advanced slowly, listening to the redwood spitting in the fire.

Assessing the situation with each step, scaling the wire fence to the back of her house, Ken landed on the smooth disloyal lawn grass that made no sound but simply caressed his bare feet and took their shape as he hopscotched over to the pot. But the cast iron stove was quite ready for Ken's challenge and had heated the oil to maximum.

Ken ran to the pot, grabbed a fork from Ms Joyce's plate stand and tried using the fork to take the chicken from the pot; from where he was, he heard the scratched sacred songs of Jim Reeves playing on her old recorder. She was bent over, taking something from her fridge with her back to him. He watched as the old woman then moved over to her kitchen sink and began washing her dirty pots and utensils.

Confident in his timing, Ken jabbed at the pieces of meat but in no time, Ms Joyce was almost at the door and on her way out. Her obesity slowed her, but as fear gripped the desperate Ken, he grabbed the half-fried meat from the hot oil with his bare hands and ran.

"Woieeee, mi hand!" Ken shouted in shock as the pain glued itself to his now-burning hand. He tossed the hot pieces of meat from one hand to the other and jumped in crazy circles on one leg then the other, as the unforgiving oil had done its damage and severely seared some of his fingers.

Ms Joyce peered wide-eyed at the spectacle, then found her voice.

"Teef! Teef! Teef!"

But slippery Ken was too fast. He had mastered the art of stealing and making a hasty getaway, and so not even her agile teenage sons could catch him, though they really tried, because it was their personal mission to hurt Ken any chance they got. Feeding on their mother's energy and dislike for the Manns over the years, these boys were Ken's nightmare even in bright daylight.

"Mama! Mama!" he shouted for Gloria, who was already on her way after hearing the commotion.

Knowing his deathly fate if caught, Ken ran barefooted through the banana trees at the back of Ms Joyce's house and jumped over the little brook that separated her property from Maas Joscelyn's. Having to climb a chain-link fence, Ken was reluctant to leave the pieces of meat behind. He stuffed what he could in his pockets and put the rest in his mouth. The hot meat burned his tongue and legs through the khaki pants as Ken jumped the fence and fell over, head first. He broke his fall on the gravel that lined the gardens at the backyard of his Uncle Darcy's house. But he could not slow down because his uncle had heard the cry of "teef!" and was waiting for the culprit with his well-sharpened machete. Not surprised to see his nephew, Darcy swung at him but missed and Ken continued his mad dash towards his house. Unsure of where Ken was, Gloria ran into Joscelyn's house and through the back door in time to see the act.

"Darcy, mind yuh chap mi pickney, so help mi God!"

By now, the sun had dipped fully behind darkening clouds – it too had to hide its face so as not to witness the spectacle. But Ken had no time to notice nature's scorn; exhausted he sat to rest for a while. Then seeing no one chasing him and hearing Gloria go at it with Darcy, Ken got up to run across the street to his house. But he didn't see the truck until it was too late; Ken didn't even hear the honking horn until he rested dumbfounded at the front of Mr McEnuff's old brown pig-laden truck, with a startled Foster in the driver's seat.

Foster had slowed, so, fortunately for him, only Ken's hands and legs were bruised when he fell from the impact.

Rolling over twice on the asphalt, more stunned from the fright than the hit, he got up and started his mad dash again. Battered and with a slowly swelling foot, Ken soon settled into hopping. Once inside his gate, he walked towards the back of his house, paying slight attention to the pain, thanks to his high threshold for it.

He reached into his pocket and pulled out the now cool bits of meat. He took a match to the still-warm coal stove and relit the embers to complete the cooking process of the scooted meat.

He found comfort on the wooden floor next to his dog, patted its head and rubbed its ribs, which were poking dangerously through its skin. From the day they arrived in Macca Tree, that dog was their only welcoming party. Licking Ken's toes for any droppings and whining when he found nothing but hardship in the creases of his master's feet, the dog turned away. Ken moved to the wooden three-step ladder at the back of the house. He did not hear the footsteps approaching before he felt the mighty whip across his back and another blow to his head. He fell to the ground with a thud; the last vision he beheld was the angry stares of Ms Joyce's sons. Ken gulped, choking on his own blood flowing from his split lip.

11. Gloria's Vengeance

The people of Macca Tree were ill-prepared for the battle of Armageddon; they were not ready to be in the midst of a mighty storm. With the fog of anger blinding Gloria's ability to reason, calm, which she never possessed, further escaped her. Having witnessed her son splayed out on the ground, writhing and pleading for her help, she screamed, "A it this. Done it done now!" as if welcoming the occasion to truly misbehave.

Running for her rusty machete, strategically placed in a hollow side of the house, unabashed curse words flew from every side of her mouth. Her hands were busy, balancing machete and a speedy change of clothes. Red was in her eyes, in her head and in the choice of her garments. A floral head tie completed her transformation; she then stood with her hands held out to both sides, the machete in her right.

Mighty Gloria – fully transformed into a comic character, drawn too loud, too perfect and too ready to destroy her make-believe world. Nothing could soothe the anger that was mounting by the minute. As if born, bred and wired for war, Gloria launched her attack, forgetting that her son, the reason for her revenge, was still lying, hurt on the ground.

The usual spectators did not wait to be called. The noise that emanated from Gloria's mouth was signal enough. Darcy, Dolly, Foster and Joyce all showed up like there was a roll call.

"Joyce! Yuh need fi pick pon somaddy yuh own size. Why yuh never come to mi if Ken did teef yuh chicken as yuh claim!" she bellowed.

"Is not a claim, I saw him with it," Darcy said with a feeble tongue, balancing on his walking stick, the remnant of a stroke. Dolly's husband was a 60-year-old heavily bearded Rastafarian with gray eyelashes, coloured by his illness.

"Oh, so Dolly let you out. You feel like a man now! Darcy, before yuh come talk to mi, go shave the broom from yuh face. From I come back here oonu have a problem wid mi. Well, I owe you nutten and is di wrong one oonu messin' wid. Si mi yah. Di whole a oonu come tek mi on now! Mi kno is long time unoo did want to do it."

Waving the machete like an uncontrollable wand, she launched her threat. As if seeking to awaken the soul of the community, Gloria's charade transformed the once quiet Macca Tree into a raging marketplace.

Her two younger children were not to be outdone. The Manns vowed to make tomorrow's headline in the *Western Mirror*.

"Is a long time now this in the making. Joyce, I wish yuh would come tek back yuh chicken. Joyce, please come tek it, because I just need an excuse fi clabba yuh."

Joyce kept her poise, safe in her yard. She flung her voice as hard as she could across the fence to her nemesis.

"Tek some responsibility, Gloria!"

Dolly added some pepper to the already heated fire. "Di juvenile delinquents what yuh have over there tormenting us long enough now. Oonu add no value to this place." She chimed in.

"What yuh just say halitosis Dolly? What yuh just say? I don't add no value?"

But Monica had shown up in her curlers and purple housedress with matching flip-flops, having heard that Gloria was at it.

"Gloria, I rebuke anything else that come from your mouth in Jesus' name! Please Gloria, be still," she lamented, hoping Gloria would come to her senses and not enrage the residents at such a critical juncture in the life of the plan.

"She look like Jackie Chang, eeh," Ron joked to Tamar as Monica tried desperately to distract Gloria by waving her arms about furiously.

"Mash-up crackers Dolly," Tamar shouted, shaking the tail of her frilled dress, much to the amusement of Gloria, who was now on patrol, marking time by pacing back and forth in her yard.

Monica's presence brought a refreshing hush in the midst. Regardless of all else, Pastor's wife had to be respected. The crowd stood still, and sense seemed to return to Gloria's head; but, just beyond Monica stood a towering figure that had crept up unnoticed.

"Gloria, that's enough," Mr McEnuff said.

Gloria stopped spewing venom long enough to acknowledge him. Kenneth had staggered into the mix as well. Looking as though he was eaten by the morning and spat out by the night, he shook off his loser garb for a while to say, "Gloria, please stop, yuh embarrassing mi again."

"What, Kenneth, what? Yuh defending them?"

Sliding back down his own spiral aided by cold sweat, Kenneth faded into the shadows once again.

"Gloria, that's enough." Mr McEnuff repeated.

"Mr Mack, I respect yuh yuh know, but know this, I don't fraid a yuh either.'

With a wave of his hand, Mr McEnuff dispersed the crowd; Monica stood still. Without an audience, Gloria had no choice but to calm. Staring at Mr McEnuff with disgust, she said, "I hear yuh, yuh know Mr Mack, but when jackass back strong them overload im hamper. I can't bear this weight anymore, is crack I just crack under pressure. When I lef Macca Tree again, I gwine throw stone behind mi."

"Gloria, you and Kenneth come by the house tomorrow. I want to talk to you both," he said.

With a heavy sigh, Gloria shook her head and walked off thinking she would use the opportunity to involve him in the scheme. Mr McEnuff was old money. Good money.

Monica's outstretched fluttering hands followed Gloria, who continued towards her house where she helped a wailing Ken into the house. Satisfied, Monica walked home.

12. Bad Seed

Going to the McEnuff plantation was always a joy for Kenneth, although he had never been inside the big white house before. At sunrise the next morning, he eagerly readied and sobered up himself as best he could.

Dancing on the head of the exploit of the previous day, Gloria was in high spirits. She stuffed herself into her brown corduroy pants and topped it off with a green and gold 'Jamaica, no problem' T-shirt. She owned the spine as she walked confidently with Kenneth on the opposite side. Familiar strangers.

From the corner of her eye, Gloria watched Kenneth, her husband of more than ten years, but she did not recognize him. A wisp of memory of intimacy past fluttered by, but, with the mission at hand, she brushed it away. She would not allow herself to be overcome by a sense of the longing that lingered deep inside her heart. Gloria would not be distracted.

Kenneth remained silent, enjoying the gardens of Joseph's coat, ten o'clocks and lilies, oblivious to the secret thoughts of his bully of a wife. He stopped briefly to pick a few buds of hibiscus from one of the well-groomed gardens lining the long McEnuff walkway. His fingers played 'she-love-me-nots' with the red petals as he went along.

"*What a frien' we have in Jesus...*" held the hum of Gloria's rasp as they ventured far beyond the iron gates and made their way towards the big white house.

"Come and join me for breakfast," Mr McEnuff said between gulps as he raised a brown-coloured ceramic mug to his head. "What type of tea would you like? I'm having some fever grass."

"I never know you drink that kind of tea, Mr Mack, I take you for a coffee type of man," Gloria chuckled.

"Give me my sarsaparilla, cerasee, lime leaf any morning; those are the teas I need to start my day; they cure any illness."

Just then the current Mrs McEnuff joined them. She was the third of them and according to the people of Macca Tree, she would certainly not be the last. But she bore the title of mother to her husband's only daughter, Tris, a feisty teenager who attended boarding school in Trelawny.

A costly black beauty, trophy wife and former Ms Jamaica, Mrs McEnuff spent most of her time in the metropolitan area of Kingston, which was far removed from her husband's simpler life in Westmoreland. One never knew when she was in Macca Tree as she was hardly ever seen. She was a rarity to Kenneth; hypnotized by her presence, he stared wide-eyed, shamelessly and almost drooling.

His eyes were fixated on her breasts which were positioned artificially high in her chest. Her perfectly arched eyebrows over squinty gray eyes were trailed by a straight nose and heart-shaped pink lips. With long black hair spilling down her upper torso, her long legs seemed to stretch for miles.

"You have a lovely wife Mr McEnuff, real pretty," Kenneth finally found his words.

"Thanks, Kenneth." Mr McEnuff was now seated at a large mahogany table in the dining hall that was adjacent to the great room.

With a hiss of her teeth, Gloria dismissed her drooling husband and shoved past him into the magnificence of the white house. Kenneth and his foolishness were for later.

All seated around the polished table under a glass candle chandelier, Mr McEnuff bowed to grace the table. Between squints, Kenneth could not contain his ogling of his former employer's wife. But boiled bananas with liver and onions, prepared by the household helper took the attention away from Mrs McEnuff. The soft bananas melted in their mouths and the well-seasoned liver made their taste buds dance.

The telephone in the great room suddenly rang, distracting the group for a moment and bringing Mrs McEnuff to her feet.

"It's Tris!" she announced. She attended to her daughter while the others continued to eat.

"What is happening with you two? I have been getting nothing but complaints. Talk to me." Mr McEnuff's voice interrupted the clanging of utensils.

"Well, Mr Mack, all I trying to be friendly, the neighbours don't want to make peace with me." Gloria finally got her chance to engage the big man.

"But, Gloria, you have a questionable past with them. So you have to give them time to warm up to you again. You stole from the community, don't forget that."

She looked to Kenneth for help. But he offered nothing, saving whatever dignity he still possessed in front of Mr McEnuff. But, not wanting to ruin her chance at getting Mr McEnuff to invest, Gloria swallowed her rising rage and held her tongue.

"I have worked too hard to keep this community out of the hands of the voracious buyers and developers who want this rich land, too hard to keep the peace and too hard to have a certain level of respect for you to act in a way contrary to the code in Macca Tree, Gloria. It's important that we have an understanding now that what happened last night cannot happen again. Macca Tree is known for, among many other things, peace and quiet, and everyone wants it to stay that way."

He paused long enough to stare his seriousness into Gloria's face.

"I like your husband, Gloria; he is a hard worker. I understand you told him not to come back here to work. Why?"

"She just don't want me happy Mr McEnuf," Kenneth chimed in shyly.

"Well, I am opening that invitation again to you Kenneth. I also understand that Foster had an unfortunate incident with your son."

"You mean him bounce him down," Gloria jabbed.

"I'll take the job, sar," Kenneth said, wanting to keep the focus positive. "I want to have enough money to give dem pickney for Christmas."

Gloria shot him a scary stare. But Mr McEnuff continued.

"I am willing to pay the doctor's fee for your son's injuries, and I also want to give you a peace offering. What can I offer you?"

Without giving Gloria a chance to respond and feeling protected in Mr McEnuff's company, Kenneth blurted, "A pig would be nice, sar; I want to start a farm yuh know, so I can be like you one day."

"OK, a pig it is then!"Mr McEnuff laughed out loud.

Overjoyed, Kenneth rose to his feet, took multiple bows to Mr McEnuff and ran, stumbling out of the house, down the incline towards the sty.

Gloria, now alone with the man, faced him square on. This is the man, her reason for coming and she was the expert in her trade. The tigress had come face to face with her prey.

"I apologize Mr Mack, I know you is the balance in this place and I will try my best not to let you down again. She sized up her victim.

He smiled. She continued. "So, sar, you hear about the thing that the church started? It's a thing called planting a seed, where you put up some money and get returns every month. They started with $5,000 each and after two months di first set a people start getting some interest yuh know."

"That sounds like a Ponzi scheme, Gloria. Why would the church do that?"

"Well, I don't know what a Ponzi scheme is, but I hear planting a seed is similar to the one Karl Hilton has in Kingston."

"You mean the one he had; that scheme crashed last week."

"What? What you mean crash? I don't understand." she said.

"Well, that type of thing cannot sustain itself, so if new people don't invest, the plan will fail."

Things were unfolding too fast for Gloria.

"So, is there any way it can work out properly? It must haffi crash?" she asked puzzled.

"Well at some point it will, because the person who usually operate these schemes don't pay out the profit they earn from the business, that's where they benefit; they only give back the new money, so when the scheme crash, they don't lose. I'm shocked that the church is involved in something like this; maybe I should talk with Pastor."

"Now Mr Mack, there is no need for that. From what I hear, the church people dem have it sort out and it will be just among them. So, I don't think this one will crash. They running it like a pardna, so people will get a kind of draw."

"Well, if it is a partner and people get only what they put in, then it should be fine. Partners always work well, especially for rural folk as many do not have bank accounts. That would be a good thing, Gloria. And if the church invests a portion of the money, a system of interest can also go with that. Who is the banker? I will have a talk with Pastor."

Gloria may not like the people of Macca Tree, Top Road or Bottom Road, but she desperately needed their respect. She wanted to tell them one day that this was her idea, that it was her who made them rich.

"Is Pastor's wife, Monica, sar."

"Oh, good, I will have a talk with Pastor to see how we can make this really work for everyone."

"So, you gwine join it, sar?"

"We will see, Gloria. We will see."

Rising from the table in a swift move, she said, "Thanks, for your time, Mr Mack, but I have to get home now to tend to the children."

Mrs McEnuff had returned to the room in time to see Gloria rising from her seat.

"Before you go, Gloria, I want you to have a look at some clothes Tris has outgrown. They are relatively new, quite fashionable. Maybe they can fit your daughter," she said pointing to some barrels in the back room.

"Thank you, Mrs Mack, but mi children don't wear second-hand clothes. We don't take tongolo from anyone."

Without giving the McEnuffs a chance to respond, she dashed out of the house, without a second thought for Kenneth, who she left behind.

Gloria heard herself praying on her way home.

"Father, is a long time we don't talk. I sorry about last night, but yuh have to help mi out with this one. Yuh know I never mean any harm; I really was trying to walk the straight and narrow with this plan. I know yuh may be upset with me, but please help the plan so it stay afloat. If yuh help mi, I won't bother you for anything else, I promise." The voice in her head trailed off in a whimper, giving way to a chatter of thoughts that she tried to ignore.

Dodging into her gate, Gloria could feel the glares from the residents, who were expecting an aftermath. But no such luck for them today; she had more important things to tend to. With an urgent need for divine intervention, Gloria breathed a sigh of relief as she safely placed her little black book in her Bible on the bed.

13. Kenneth's Redemption

Kenneth, who was now on the farm with Cheddy and Tiger, was oblivious to Gloria's woes, glad to be a working man again. Boasting of his newly acquired pig, he high-fived the men and settled into his job.

They sat on hardened dirt under the shade of a sprawling almond tree with shedding brownish-yellow and green leaves. The four men traded bar jokes while wasting a perfectly good morning.

With his wife at home, Mr McEnuff had taken some much-needed time off from the farm and left his men to tend to his business.

"So yuh cooking pork for Christmas?" Foster grinned.

"No, I going to start a farm, rear mi own pigs, so I can make my own money."

Tiger and Cheddy issued Kenneth a unified uneasy, quizzical chuckle.

"Aye, leave him alone," Foster jumped to Kenneth's defense. "Kenneth, I owe yuh a apology, I never mean to bounce down Ken; him come outta nowhere, run right in the truck."

"I know you wouldn't do that Foster. But I also want to say sorry for how Gloria was behaving. She really did shame me," Kenneth added, staring into space.

"So, why yuh make she talk to yuh so, Kenneth? Yuh is a man yuh know; yuh must show har who is boss," Tiger got up and dusted off his behind.

"I is man enuff. Just leave my wife to me. Mind your business." Kenneth picked up a piece of twig from the ground beside him and doodled in the dirt.

Changing the touchy subject, Foster said, "Speaking of making money, oonu hear about the plant-a-seed saving down by the church? All of Macca Tree talking about it."

Everyone nodded except Kenneth. Foster did not miss a beat in bringing him up to speed with its workings.

"Planting a seed huh?" Kenneth massaged his beard as if in deep thought.

The thought of telling Gloria's secret ran through and away from his mind. The urge to continue the conversation erased itself from him. He wasn't feeling chatty anymore. In his mind, he relived the day they were chased out of Macca Tree because Gloria had taken the residents' partner money; Kenneth cringed involuntarily, knowing he had to stop this one in its tracks.

The men bantered on around him: "We just waiting until it start again; Foster inviting us to join. Wi money ready," Tiger said. Still Kenneth stroked his beard absentmindedly until finally disturbed by the cackling of a mother fowl, followed by a sprinkling of baby chicks.

Returning his attention to the group, Kenneth was somewhat startled by the fast and furious Tiger who had chased the fowls down the hillside.

"Bwoy, di devil really find work fi idle hands; why yuh doing that Tiger; what if Mr McEnuff see yuh? Him wud think yuh mad."

"Well him not here, so if him know, a yuh a go tell him. Yuh is a informer Kenneth?"

"This is how him terrorize the animals." Foster added his annoyance and felt a kick to his leg, as the returning Tiger was not amused.

The men laughed it off, but Kenneth, relieved that the discussion had changed course, still didn't think it was funny. In that moment, something moved deep inside him, as if warning him that both men were omens of sorts. As he concentrated on his company, he faced the hard fact that he really knew nothing about the two men Mr McEnuff had introduced him to the first day he had come to work on the farm.

With their hats forever hiding their faces, Cheddy and Tiger were ghosts to the community; no one really knew what they looked like. Coming out only at nights, they avoided questions and were allowed to move about at will.

"Well I going to the fields to look around. It's been a while since I was here. See yuh later, Foster." Kenneth took refuge from the eyes of the other men.

The tangy flavour of tangerines he had picked from a dwarf tree at the foot of the incline was perfect and Kenneth groaned in appreciation of the sweetness.

For the rest of the day, he tried to play catch-up, overworking himself in the process. He took pride in washing the sties and tending to the squealing pigs, fighting the ever-present urge to find a bar. Thinking ahead, he dreaded going home because he knew the matter of the plan had to be addressed, but talking to Gloria was like digging through a mountain with a toothpick; with her, the more he dug the more he had to dig. But the earlier talk with Mr McEnuff and even the unwarranted advice from Tiger gave him a certain amount of strength; so much so that he believed he could command the same amount of respect from Gloria as Mr McEnuff had.

Walking home that evening, he braced himself for the task at hand. Sty-stink, he had gone to Sweet River for a swim. Now clean and fresh in the same dirty clothes, Kenneth was greeted by his children at their gate. It was the first time in a while he was seeing them while sober. Tamar's hair was unkempt, Ron was shirtless and Ken, still hopping, was without shoes. Kenneth hugged each of his children with renewed joy at finally being able to look them in the eye, knowing he was going to be able to buy them gifts for Christmas and make up for lost time. He already knew what to buy each. Tamar was getting a new dress and a doll; Ron would get a real bat and ball and Kenneth would get a lovely pair of shoes. He was also thinking of sending them back to school, maybe after the Easter break, but he hadn't made up his mind as yet. For the time being, though, Kenneth wanted Ken to join him on the farm and learn from Mr McEnuff, just as he was doing.

Making his way to the house, Kenneth looked around at the grass which had returned to its move-in-day height. Resolving to take his machete to it and show Gloria he could do manly things, he walked on.

"Joscelyn in there, yuh know daddy," Ken cautioned. "Mamma cook and him eating."

The anger rose and raged engulfed Kenneth. But his beef was not with Joscelyn. He stormed past the older man seated in his kitchen, careful to miss each pothole in the floor, and went directly to Gloria. The house reeked of ripe bananas and naseberries since, like a reaper of harvest he did not sew, Ken had done his daily routine of gathering what he could from wherever.

On nearing Gloria's room, Kenneth took in a deep gulp of air, pulling in courage from the atmosphere, and pounded on her door.

"Is who that and what yuh want?" she demanded.

"Is me, Gloria; Kenneth, I need to talk to you. Why Joscelyn in mi house, on mi chair of all places?"

"Oh, so you finally remember me. What? Mrs McEnuff refuse yuh?"

"I not joking, Gloria, I coming into the room now."

With that he barged in on her.

"Gloria, yuh will stop these kind of foolishness yuh know. I have feelings too. I don't disrespect yuh. It bad yuh go to his house, but why him must come to mine?"

Gloria did not flinch. She was unmoved by Kenneth's small disturbance.

"What yuh want Kenneth? Talk fast mek I get back to what mi a do."

"Yuh is my wife, Gloria," he retorted.

"Well, maybe if I had long hair and a pretty face, yuh would treat mi like yuh wife," she said.

"I love mi children, Gloria, and it is for that reason only I don't regret you. But know this, if yuh did even have long hair and pretty face and stay how yuh stay, I would still have a problem wid yuh."

Fighting the urge to reach for his flask of rum, still sitting on a shelf in the kitchen, Kenneth steadied his hands on the remains of a cigarette he had reserved in his pocket. He pretended to pull puffs from the unlit butt into his lungs.

"Get him out of mi chair!" He shouted.

Kenneth's voice ripped through years of inhibition. His words penetrated her head, reverberated in her heart and bloated her face. Pushing past him, she felt his resistance and knew he was dead serious. She went to the kitchen and dismissed a protesting Joscelyn. Unbeknown to Kenneth, she had also won a small victory because she detected a bit of jealousy in his reaction, as was her undertaking.

"Go home, nuh man," she urged amidst his buts and whys.

The children were ecstatic to say the least; watching him go was a small victory for all of them. Jeering a jaded Joscelyn, Ken hopped on one foot around him, mimicking his walk while the other two ran to open the wire gate.

"Have a good night now, Maas Joscelyn," Ken laughed, "and don't come back here."

Back inside, Gloria was somewhat subdued.

"What yuh want, Kenneth?"

"Is your plan dem have down the church?"

"What if I say it is?"

"Then I would tell yuh to stop it now. I not running leave mi life again for you, Gloria. If this thing don't work out me and the children staying and yuh alone leaving."

"So why yuh think it wouldn't work out? Yuh hear something?" she was apprehensive.

"Look, I don't know much about it. I just know that you and people money don't mix well."

"Don't worry about it. People lining up to join in; it cyaa fail."

"So, how yuh get Monica to do it for yuh? Foster tell mi sey is she read it out in church. Yuh and dat cousin of yours is two bad duppy yuh nuh."

With a dismissive wave of her hand she ordered a reluctant Kenneth out of her room and slammed her door shut. Removing the bit of cigarette from his lips, he shouted through the locked door. "I is the man in this house, Gloria; yuh will show mi di respect I deserve!"

She shouted back: "I showing yuh it already. This is all di respect yuh will get from mi!"

Turning on his heels, Kenneth went to the dimly lit kitchen and dished himself a chipped bowl of the cold lumpy cornmeal porridge Gloria left seeped up, in the coal-blackened Dutch pot.

It offered little comfort to his stomach. The flask of rum beckoned to him from across the room, but ignoring the urge, Kenneth went on to the verandah, putting distance between himself and his tempter.

What a day, he thought. He had a job he loved and putting Gloria in her place was priceless. The thought of Tiger and Cheddy tickled him a bit, but with the children now inside, Kenneth knew his family was safe. So, closing his eyes, he soon fell into an uneasy dose.

Waking up a little after 9:00 p.m., he heard Gloria combing the house for her children. Satisfied that everyone was in bed she headed for the veranda and came across Kenneth.

"Di ole fool sleeping on the verandah again like a watchdog. Is who him think coming in here?" Gloria muttered to herself as she tiptoed across the hall so as not to make the creak. Sneaking past Kenneth that night, Gloria was as quiet as a hush. She had to see Monica.

Unwilling to accept that her husband had put some fear into her, she wanted to ensure that nothing would go as he predicted. Once she passed the barking dogs on the street, she ignored Tiger and Cheddy holding their usual corner beneath the disguise of their wide-brimmed hats. She entered Pastor's yard cautiously and edged up to Monica's bedroom, which she shared with the man of the cloth.

Armed with some pebbles she had picked up along the way, she took careful aim at the French window.

The tinkling sound was signal enough for Monica, who was already on edge. She peered through the drawn curtains. Ensuring that the coast was clear of Pastor's prying eyes, she rushed to the front door.

"Is what now, Gloria; all is well?"

"All is well wid me. But I don't think all is well wid di plan. We need to talk."

Jumping into her shoes, an eager Monica rushed out of the house in a see-through robe, displaying her fancy undergarments.

"What going on, Gloria?"

"'Yuh remember I tell yuh sey is a man name Karl Hilton I get di idea from? Well, him plan just crash."

"Mercy!" Monica mouthed quietly.

"Not only that, but McEnuff wid him nuff self want to talk to yuh husband about di plan."

"What? So who tell him about it?" Monica asked.

"I don't see how that important." Gloria said. "The point is, him know now. I tell him sey the church running it like a pardna."

"A what dis yuh put mi inna, Gloria?" Monica bemoaned.

"Look, Monica. We stick to di plan. It's simple. Prepare yuh husband fi di McEnuff enquiry. Tell him to tell McEnuff is a pardna. Him will do anything yuh sey."

"Alright, I will see it done. But we have to talk some more on this. I have to go now, but I'll come by tomorrow for the regular prayer session."

"Alright, tomorrow then," Gloria said and departed a lot lighter on her feet.

14. A Seed Becomes a Tree

Weeks floated by, pulling along the due date for the congregation to be paid their second tranche of returns. On the day of jubilee, the street was paved with new investors patiently positioned in a line leading to the church for a chance to be a part of the God plan. Waiting in line, the prospects fanned themselves with hats and bits of the newspaper they brought from a vendor who plied the community.

Vendors capitalized on the occasion coming out to display an array of fruits, cooked food and other items hoping to attract some of the money from the investors. Young and old had heard the word.

With no marketing, Monica was surprised at the response, and with a big smile on her face she welcomed all, pronouncing a blessing on their lives. Dressed in one of her signature bosom-baring, bottom-emphasizing outfits, she issued hugs, lifted children, shook hands and planted kisses. On a normal day this would seem like overdone insanity, but today, Monica was moving in the Spirit as she declared God was controlling her every move.

Too good to be true, people turned up from all walks of life, almost tripling the amount of the initial investors. Not ones to fall back on their word, Tiger and Cheddy joined the fast-growing queue. Also in the area was Kenneth, who, dressed in his khaki sty garb, had momentarily left the farm to witness the happenings for himself.

Everyone was present at church and so Kenneth was alone walking along the desolate Macca Tree spine. In the cutting heat, the zinc roofs took pleasure basking in the sun, blinding Kenneth as he went along. But he was curious because next to the crusade, it was the first time Kenneth had seen so many people at church in this quiet community; he smiled to think that not even the prophecy of God's return in 2000 had yielded so many willing souls.

Shaking his head in dismay, Kenneth thought that the church had outdone itself by allowing Monica and Gloria's arrangement to materialize and flourish. Then suddenly, as if echoing his thoughts, the day quickly turned windy causing frightened dogs to lend their howling voices to the gust. The trees cried as the wind tossed them from side to side and the sun, though in her glory, suddenly had no effect. Rain should follow, but there was none; there was no shower of blessing for the Macca Tree folks that day.

Toying with his beard, Kenneth watched as Tiger and Cheddy exited the church laughing as though they just won the lottery, stopping too long to embrace a too-eager Monica. Kenneth turned away, hiding the disgust that etched itself on his face.

Walking past the crowd at the church's entrance, Kenneth saw Monica hard at work with her helpers singing and dancing in praise to God for his blessing; the God plan was indeed a success. But, in the midst of all the gallivanting, he noted that there was no sign of Gloria. Somehow, he found consolation in her absence. But Gloria had no need to be present, having already instructed Monica to turn no one away but collect every dollar and every cent. This Gloria had done at their last supposed prayer meeting when she used the opportunity to convince a worrying Monica that everything would work out as scheduled.

"Once the next set join up we can basically take our pay. Yuh say yuh have $350,000. Well that a ours; just tek a portion fi di church building fund. A ours that because who a come next a go pay the set before and so on and on and on. And with the crowd getting larger each time, we will always have an excess," Gloria assured her. "Just make sure sey your husband tell Mr McEnuff that is a big partner unoo running." Trusting Gloria's street smarts, Monica had left the Manns' house with hope.

The extravagant turnout that day was an even bigger conviction that they were proceeding on the right path. Looking right through Kenneth, Monica counted the cash and ignored the daggers he threw at her through his stares.

Despite the change in the atmosphere, the celebration continued and intensified when the congregation received their expected incentive. A wail of thanksgiving erupted to the skies, loud enough for the clouds to dance to the singsong voices as they raised their thanksgiving towards the heavens. Heading home that fulfilling evening, the people of Macca Tree continued with their scant regard for Gloria, who was stationed at her gate taking in the merriment.

"Imagine getting this every month from the little seed wi sew," Dolly said to Joyce. "I'm thinking of increasing my seed yuh know."

"God bless Sister Monica," Joyce replied.

God bless me, Gloria thought. Anticipating the horror on their faces when they learn of her involvement, Gloria burst out in vulgar chuckles as if to announce her presence while bending over to hold her belly. Behind her the three children played hopscotch in the yard, making enough noise to compete with the local Unity Primary School.

Evening had taken hold of the community, retiring the pregnant day; in the cool of the moment, Gloria watched them for a while, but was jolted by an annoyed Kenneth stepping past her without any salutation and heading to the house. Returning from work, Kenneth was trailed by the anxious children, much to his satisfaction. Charming them with fruits from the McEnuff's farm, he was intent on ignoring Gloria, who needed no explanation for his behaviour; she knew what the source of his indignation was. But with no intention of pulling the plug on her plans, she turned her back to them and continued to be amused by the talkative Joyce and Dolly.

15. Cover-up and Revelations

The chatter surrounding the God plan was so loud that Mr McEnuff heard it from his house. Bent on finding out what exactly was happening in his precious Macca Tree, two days later, he made good on his word and visited the pastor. Monica's husband, who was already briefed of the promised visit, opened the gate to greet Mr McEnuff.

Facing each other, both men had nothing in common. Where Mr McEnuff was tall, Pastor was short; where the pastor was stout, the farmer was slender. Whereas Mr McEnuff was in command, the pastor was a puppeteer's pet personified – a good student, seated at the front of Monica's class over the few years they had been married. Never wanting to disappoint her by going against her requests, the pastor always did as Monica commanded – even marrying her after she made an impromptu marriage proposal to him two months after his ailing first wife died.

A much younger Monica had sealed that deal by telling him that the Lord relayed their union in a vision; having no children, the pastor gained a daughter and a wife in one fell swoop, thus making Monica the First Lady of the community. Moving from the capital, Savanna-la-Mar, where she resided with her aunt, Monica relocated to the community-hosted two-bedroom house reserved for the head of the church and his family. Over time, she used her wiles to master the art of manipulation, so her husband had grown accustomed to being played, never wanting to be detached from the strings she pulled.

"Welcome Mr McEnuff. To what do I owe the pleasure of your presence on this wonderful day?" Pastor asked, dressed in his black suit and white collar.

The day was indeed wonderful; Macca Tree had returned to its regular activities, graced by all the elements nature could provide for an unforgettable day. Lloyd Lovindeer's 'Pocomania Day' rode on the wind from a nearby radio, but was suddenly drowned out by the gospel music of the Grace Thrillers. Seeing Mr McEnuff, Monica felt the need to pump up the volume on her player, putting her acclaimed spirituality on full display.

"Well I hear about a little thing the church have going on down there. I just come to hear a little bit more about it."

"Come sit with me on the verandah, Mr Mack. This may take a while." There were four chairs and a knitted hammock from which Mr McEnuff could choose, all placed below hanging flowers. Pastor was ready to deliver his message; Monica, serving lemonade from a glass Ewer, had joined the men on the covered entrance.

"You remember my wife, Monica," Pastor said gesturing to her.

"Yes, of course," Mr McEnuff replied, turning his attention to her, "how are you, my dear?"

Blushing, she nodded her acknowledgement. Monica always enjoyed the attention of an older man.

Continuing his persuasion, Pastor said, "I guarantee you, it's not a Ponzi scheme, Mr Mack. What can I say, the Lord laid a plan on Monica's heart and many will reap rewards if they are obedient to his call."

"Well I don't intend to get between you and your god, Pastor, but this thing has the potential to get out of control, I have seen it happen."

Monica had now affixed herself to Pastor's side, egging him on as he spoke. But for anyone who knew them, this was not strange behaviour. Monica was his devil and his angel, flipping roles at will to shape him for different occasions. Unknown to Gloria, it was Monica who convinced the pastor

to get involved when she had taken the partner money
three years ago. Audaciously trying hard to hide her part
in the robbery, she insisted day and night that her husband
instigate the community to rise up against Gloria and
her family, sending them back to Kenneth's birth parish,
Trelawny. Like a persistent mosquito, Monica lived in his
ear until he gave in and banished the Manns from church.
Once prominent members of the flock, Gloria and Kenneth
became fugitives from Macca Tree in a heartbeat.

"I tell you, Mr Mack, it was like an angel spoke to mi
clearly. I got the revelation like God Himself was talking to
mi. I couldn't turn my back on God; He has been too good
to me." Monica chimed in.

Monica continued her sermon to Mr McEnuff. The lounge
chair she had perched herself on was just one of the many
pieces of furniture the Manns had in their yellow board
house before the house and furniture were sold to repay
the stolen partner money, back then, with negligible regard
for the law.

Being the banker for the community partner, Gloria
was accountable for over $600,000 when her mother fell
ill from cancer. Being the sole caretaker and burdened
with the countless treatments and long trips to Kingston
over the infamous Spur Tree Hill, within months her funds
were exhausted. But Gloria had a plan B and using Monica
as collateral, she had given her a third of the money. In
the height of her distress, Gloria decided to buy Monica's
silence whilst making a deal that she would use the church
funds to replenish the partner money before anyone knew;
Gloria intended to repay the church in small amounts. Not
one to pass on money, Monica caved; not wanting to be a
part of such scheming, she confessed. Once it was leaked
that the money had been stolen, a raging mob descended
on the Manns on a cold winter night. Their iciness was
echoed among the barking mongrels that also seem to be

demanding that the Manns pay up. But there was no money to repay.

The only thing of value belonging to the Manns was their house and its contents. Pastor instructed that these things be sold to compensate the community. Without an active conscience, Monica watched as Joscelyn, who had the biggest hand in the partner, used horse and cart to move the Manns' house over to his property. It was one of the darkest days in Macca Tree, the first and last of its kind. Paying over money to some residents, giving furniture to others, Joscelyn added Kenneth and Gloria's structure to his one bedroom house, upgrading it instantly to four. Still, Monica never wavered.

Convinced then, as now, that she was doing the right thing, Monica continued on her rampage of reason to Mr McEnuff, "This will be nothing like what Gloria did pull off Mr Mack. I am a decent law-abiding God-fearing woman. The people trust me and I won't let them down."

Changing the subject, she added, "So, I hear Kenneth working for you again."

"Yes, he is a fine worker; I have no problems with him."

"Agree. He is very reliable." She added.

But Monica never cared about Kenneth or Gloria. She never cared when Gloria told her that she visited Joscelyn just to get a feel of the house that she poured blood sweat and tears into building. She never cared when Gloria told her that sitting at the bus shed was the only way she was able to see the spot where her house was built. She never cared that Dolly, Gloria's best friend had abandoned her for fear of being associated with a criminal, or that Kenneth never spoke to his brother again after the entire community turned against him. A testament to ignorance, Gloria and Kenneth had indeed suffered the wrath of Macca Tree, thanks to Monica.

Her conniving nature hit its peak and she smiled when she saw Mr McEnuff shifting to leave.

"Well, I hear that you have it under control, so I won't dig deeper. I know you folks have a lot to do, so I'll take my leave," Mr McEnuff said as he departed without getting closure on the matter. Relieved to see him go, Monica used her best voice to bid him farewell.

"So will we see you in church on Sunday?" She asked.

Laughing, he replied, "Look for me with one eye open."

With that he left. Strolling along the spine, his ears rang from the bevy of good mornings that were thrown at him. If Macca Tree had a Don, he would be Mr McEnuff because he realized early in life that creating his own wealth meant owning the entire community, and acted accordingly. If a money plan was in existence in Macca Tree, he would have to be the benefactor and the beneficiary.

When Kenneth sought his advice three years ago on how to appease the cheated neighbours, it was he who advised him to sell anything he could to compensate them. Having had nothing but his house and unknown to Gloria, Kenneth had gone to the pastor and indicated that he should sell the house, because he intended to move his family back to Trelawny, feeling responsible for the savage state of Macca Tree.

As the author of the sale, McEnuff ensured he was positioned to exact interest from the purchaser for what he considered to be sound advice.

But Kenneth's decision to sell the house backfired on his family as he lost his wife's respect because she felt he hadn't fought hard enough to keep their possessions.

A former fisherman in Bluefield, Kenneth reluctantly sold his fishing pots and speedboat he had named 'Gloria' so he could provide for them once they moved. Never intending to return to Macca Tree, an ashamed Kenneth did so at Gloria's insistence after three years, and took up residence in the old forgotten house. Initially belonging to Mr McEnuff's family, the premises was abandoned years ago when Mr McEnuff moved to his current property. The house has since then been occupied by many, even the drifting insane. But once the Manns returned to Macca Tree, it became their refuge, and having no real problem with the family, Mr McEnuff allowed their invasion and even employed Kenneth.

He remembered when Kenneth and Darcy moved to Macca Tree – one a fisherman, the other a farmer. The two men's wives became best friends over time. By the time he heard that Kenneth had sold his belongings and relocated, it was too late for an undoing; but Kenneth had gained his respect for that bold statement and respect was not something Mr McEnuff issued unwarranted.

16. Blooming Seeds, Dying Trees

Time passed, and as Gloria predicted, there was continuous and more overwhelming responses to the calls for new instalments. Repeat and new investors tailing on the whirlwind of proven success, chased the power money wielded. Wanting to quench the dire thirst of greed, they formed a rambunctious crowd descending on the church. The green and white striped tent was pitched to provide additional shelter due to the fluctuating weather. The choir came together as spur-of-the-moment entertainment. Pastor busied himself moving through the crowd, preaching mini-sermons as he went along in a bid to capture lost souls and balance the commercial intake of the church.

With each person inviting others to join, Monica increased her support staff twofold. In fact, the entire church community was in full gear, issuing payments to some and taking new investments from others; no longer was this a God plan, it was a straight money-making scheme. God had given them money and the money had become their god.

Monica and Gloria were unperturbed and the latter soon forgot the worries Mr McEnuff and Kenneth represented. Now a secret nouveau riche, Gloria did not want to bring attention to herself by expediting the house-building process. Despite the flow of money along the spine, the only concrete house in Macca Tree remained that of Mr McEnuff. But Gloria was fixing to change that. Waiting for the appropriate moment to approach Tom about purchasing a lot of land, Gloria bided her time. But her thoughts did not mirror those of Kenneth who daily fought a losing battle petitioning her to cease and control the craziness. She was now consumed with the delusion of grandeur and newly acquired self-importance.

"Don't try to make your problem mine," was all Kenneth managed to squeeze from her.

Kenneth felt as though he was steering a ship through a glacier of icebergs while walking through Macca Tree. It was quite apparent to him that the surroundings in that community had changed. Lush green leaves no longer waltzed in the blistering weather, and even the lawn grass which usually invited all to share its velvety lushness now had hills of intruding red ants.

Kenneth took note of changes in the trees which once flourished; now they appeared to be withering from an invasion of duck ants. With no fields of grazing cattle, Top Road became barren; and then the swamp of Bottom Road dried up into a winding pathway of dust and parched river stones. Brilliant scenery caved in to the desolate surroundings. Lush farmlands along the curves of Macca Tree became desert flatlands on a snaky road bordered by slopes of boulders and scrawny trees. Suddenly, the stray dogs no longer stood out, but were a perfect match for the fast-deteriorating environment.

All the familiar comforts in Macca Tree were long gone, replaced by greed. Droopy vegetation gave up their place in the world as they push themselves downward to the earth, waving goodbye in the wind and disappearing into dried dead spots. The asphalt road had not met a broom in months and the discarded cardboard boxes emptied of newly bought furnishings took their place among dried leaves and other debris in the roadway. Kenneth slowed on one of his treks up the road to take in the social decay. He blamed Gloria and her cursed plan for Macca Tree's demise.

Uncaring, she was on cloud nine.

"So, how much wi have now?" Gloria asked Monica with glee.

"Well. After the last batch wi have millions, Glor! Millions. I can't believe I did doubt yuh."

"Mek dat be a lesson to yuh. Wi is a great team."

"So Gloria, yuh don't tink is time wi take di money to a bank?"

"No sah. Nobody coming to yuh yaad. Who would dare try thief from a pastor. Plus, nobody know where wi keeping di money; dem just waan dem interest."

One the brains, the other the beauty; neither the voice of reason. Neither heeded the wisdom of Mr Mack, who, at his wife's request, had left the community for a few weeks to partake in a fundraising event in Kingston. This would be one of the many he attended all over the island.

Leaving Kenneth in charge of his property, he felt secure in his choice, knowing Kenneth would keep his promise to watch over his flourishing acres which was the only place not disturbed by the Macca Tree plague of a plan. Unsure of when he would return, Mr McEnuff left strict instructions.

"Mr Mack," a too-curious Kennneth could no longer contain the burning question, "is where Tiger and Cheddy come from? If yuh don't mind mi asking sar."

"I met them in Frome, by the sugar factory. They asked for work and I took them here."

"So, yuh don't know anything else about them sar?"

"No, I'm afraid that's it Kenneth. What, is something wrong?"

Kenneth shook his head.

"Kenneth, if something's the matter, you best tell me now. I will be gone for a while. I'd hate to think that I brought trouble to Macca Tree."

"No sar, all is well. I never mean to frighten yuh. I was just...amm...what's the big word?"

"Curious?"

Smiling, Kenneth replied, "Yes, sar."

"Well, call me if anything."

With that, Mr McEnuff drove off in his black Mercedes.

Tooting at the gate, he continued in his seat of luxury, hugging the unbushed, garbage-strewn road, smooth like a snake along the 'esses'.

Kenneth smiled his way round the farm like a child with a brand-new toy. A feeling of novelty engulfed him. It was Ken's second week with him on the farm. Scared to let his older son out of his sight, he kept his eyes on Tiger and Cheddy and kept the boy close at all times. No time like the present, Kenneth decided to have a heart-to-heart with his son.

Sitting under the shady almond tree, he looked at Ken whose eyes followed Tiger and Cheddy as they carried out their chores. There was no hiding the fact that he wanted to join the more youthful bunch. Foster slept on the ground a few feet away from them. With his bar days firmly rooted in his past, Kenneth strived at having his father-skills bear fruit. He sat trying to block the vision of Tiger and Cheddy. Having gone to the barber recently, his low hair was darker than usual, reaching just past his chin to flow into a moustache. His piercing gray eyes tried to hold Ken's attention while his soft voice tumbled over a prickly silhouette of spiky growth stretching over his bony cheeks.

"Ken, right now I don't have much to give yuh. I know I is not a good father, but I will try to do mi best."

He paused, toying with his hand, trying to get the boy's full attention.

"Ken, I want yuh to stop stealing; a real man don't take what is not his."

"But, Dada, mi only taking things from di people dem who did take our things," a now-attentive Ken replied.

"Ken, dem take wi tings 'cause we did take from dem first; but I don't want to talk about that now. One day, I will tell yuh everything. For now, I just want yuh to stop teefing."

Impulsive Ken was in deep thought, then he nodded his head in agreement.

"Ken, people say I is not a man, but the things I did fi mi family a lot of them wouldn't do. Sometimes in di bars mi not drunk; a just listen and watch. Yuh see, Ken, sometimes you need fi step back fi see things a different way, and mi learn nuff, Ken. I may never get the respect I want in this place 'cause mi may nuh able fi change people's mind about mi, but a want to make a difference in yuh. Mi go through nuff inna life, Ken, but it all lead to dis, yuh know. Life funny, yuh know, Ken. What I did want is not what I have now, but I have to just accept it. Gloria and I don't have bad mind; wi jus mess up. And she love yuh, yuh know; she just show it funny. Yuh know I give yuh mi name 'cause I did want yuh to be just like yuh ole man, but a hope you better than mi when yuh have kids. I want yuh to be a good boy and look out fi yuh brother and sister because family important, Ken. Yuh hear mi, boy?"

"Yes, Dada. But why yuh telling mi all dis now?"

"Because I don't want yuh messing around with Tiger and Cheddy; I feel dem is bad news, Ken and a trying to set yuh straight. Promise mi yuh won't join dem company. That's not why I carry yuh here. I carry yuh here to learn."

"But dem is already mi friends, Dada."

"Yuh hear mi, Ken?" Kenneth asked sternly.

"Yes, Dada," the startled boy replied.

For the rest of that day, Ken followed his father around like a puppy on a leash. Empowered by his responsibility, Kenneth took pride in his overseeing duties – double-checking the locks and doors, counting the fruits on trees, mowing the already low lawn, and checking on the animals.

He went about his days like a rooster with a crown. Not to be outdone in her endeavours, Gloria counted her portion of the cash behind her doors. Wetting her finger with saliva, she buried herself in hundred-dollar, five-hundred dollar and even one thousand-dollar bills. The dirty smell of money was no deterrent as she stuffed her pillows and mattress with it. Dreaming only of more, she was content with her plan. With no Tom McEnuff to judge her and Kenneth distracted being at his property, Gloria enjoyed sweet freedom.

17. Two Robberies: One Day

The humid and torrid effects of the tropics were piercing in Macca Tree during the summer. Having received his sow from Mr McEnuff and purchasing all needed material for his sty, Kenneth decided to take an afternoon off from the farm to build the structure. He invested all the money he had in this venture. As the sty took shape, he was ecstatic, to say the least. Relaying his pending absence to Foster, Kenneth was not surprised when the older man expressed discomfort with the idea of being left alone to work with Tiger and Cheddy.

"I think yuh should wait until Mr Mack come back yuh tek di time off Kenneth," he said. "Dem always a fool round mi like is a joke, but I don't like it. Mi always tell dem sey 'what is joke to unoo is death to me', but dem just laugh it off, sey mi too saaf."

"Is only for a few hours, Foster," Kenneth replied. "Mi already lock up everything and wata wat fi get wata. Just lock the gate later when yuh leaving and come give mi di gate key."

Sitting under the almond tree, they looked across the lawn at the younger men staring back at them.

"Young people these days different, een Foster," Kenneth said.

"Yea, I 'member inna my days bwoy a bwoy and man a man; respect did due to elders. As a bwoy, my fun was jumping over drains, playing marble or spinning gigs."

Not wanting to add to his frustration, Kenneth tried to steer the discussion in another direction, "And yuh better nuh drop inna dat drain, yuh know Foster, or is a beating dat." Both men laughed out loud. Ken, who sat with them, smiled as he raked a piece of broken twig across the rock-hard ground.

"Inna dem days, wi birthday cake was a bulla, yuh know, Ken. Wi neva know 'bout icing. Wi neva have soda; wi did have soft drinks," Kenneth continued.

The trip down memory lane was fun and exhilarating.

"Yuh memba how wi used to bathe and go inside early fi hear duppy story, Foster? Dem time deh, yuh fraid fi guh back out 'cause yuh nuh waan rolling calf or three-foot horseman catch yuh, yuh know. If yuh nuh bathe before the story, yu nah bathe that night." Laughter erupted as the two older men high-fived to the memory.

"I don't know about yuh, Kenneth, but I used to mek mi own slippers from cardboard and cloth, yuh know."

"Yes, man, mi did duh dat too. Wear it go school sometime to enuh, Ken. We neva know 'bout bus yuh know; wi walk to and from school. Dem time deh, mi used to save mi buss-mi-jaw sweetie dem fi when mi a walk home," Kenneth said.

"Yeh, man. And when wi walking home, sometime wi do fi purpose wet up inna di rain."

"Yes, mi memba, Foster. Wi used to tear out wi book leaf dem and mek boat fi sail inna di rainwater."

"Wi used to hop on pon mule and cart when it a pass wid cane. The cartman used to use him whip and slap wi, but from wi get a piece a cane wi wudda tek di beating."

Laughing and brushing away falling tears with the back of his hand, Foster rolled over on the ground. Memories had lifted their spirits. Telling Cheddy and Tiger about his early departure was less dramatic for Kenneth, as both men shrugged away the importance of the information.

Without a challenge and on a mission, Kenneth left the property.

Walking home with Ken, Kenneth shaded his squinty eyes with his hand, stained with McEnuff's red dirt. Ken was fully clothed in T-shirt and jeans with flip-flops, thanks to Gloria who had gone shopping for the children. Kenneth hoped for rain for many reasons. He wanted to see the community connected again, even if it meant by water. And then the earth was so thirsty, cracking open in too many places.

Heading inside his house, Kenneth followed the sweet smell of stewed chicken to the kitchen. Thick steam emitting from the meat in the open pot on the brand new gas stove with oven Gloria had acquired, made his mouth water. Kenneth thought of dipping his teeth deep into the moist chicken chewing and swallowing hard. Eating only fruits all day, a well-cooked meal was a welcome thought. He even thought of the sweet gravy sticking to his hand after resting his fork to the side of his plate, to crush the season-soaked bones.

Dancing and singing to retro dancehall music on her new component set, Gloria failed to see or hear her husband or her son enter the house. Watching her dance ska to dancehall music, Kenneth was amused at how beautifully lousy a dancer she was. But she was happy, and though he did not approve of the source of her joy, he knew there was nothing he could have done to make her this happy. Whether or not he wanted to admit it, Kenneth also knew Gloria needed validation after her past failures. Glee oozing from her pores meant a happy house for all, so Kenneth rested his criticisms and enjoyed the show. Hands clapping, feet stomping, voice cracking under the pressure of reaching for a too-high note, Gloria was in her element.

But, with the evening drawing nearer, Kenneth had to proceed with the matter at hand. With the help of Ken and Ron, he had dug the foundation days before and now all that was left was the actual laying of blocks. Again with the help of his sons, Kenneth outdid himself that evening. The sty was now a reality. Tired, he leaned back and rested his head against a tree stump in the backyard. The boys had left him to eat dinner, at his request, and soon after, his eyelids grew heavy with slumber. Within minutes, he lost the battle with sleep. When he awoke, hours had passed, and still Foster had not come by with the key.

Heading to the community hotspots, including the bars, in hopes of finding Foster, Kenneth felt no worries. But when Foster was missing from both bars, he headed back to the agricultural estate to see if he could locate him. As night drew closer, Kenneth approached the driveway, to the house, looked around for any sign of Foster, but saw none. Finally he went to the back of the house and there he found the older man, dazed, looking as though he was just in a car crash. He rested against the house looking down at his body, but seemingly having no real control of it. Kenneth saw that Foster was in pain, blood was coming from his nose and mouth as he grumbled to him. Bruised, busted and banged up, he clawed his way towards a startled Kenneth who rushed to his side.

"Is what do yuh Foster?" he panicked.

Gibberish stumbled from Foster's bloodied lips.

"Foster, talk to mi nuh. What happened?"

"Dem rob di place," he whispered. "Mi was locking up when dem jump mi and beat mi up. Dem cut the grill and go tek what dem want from the house."

"Who, Foster?"

"I don't know. Dem put a crocus bag over mi face and one a dem stay wid mi fi mek sure mi nuh take it off and den run off."

"Come mek I carry yuh home, Foster."

Getting a wheelbarrow outside a nearby shed, Kenneth placed Foster into it and struggling under his weight, wheeled him home. Once inside Foster's gate, they were greeted by his sons and Joyce, who came out shouting at the top of her voice.

"Is Gloria do this?" she asked.

Gloria's name alone was enough for all to come from their houses and on to the spine.

"No, Joyce, is not she this time," Foster said.

"I taking yuh to di hospital now, now, now," Joyce said.

"I OK Joyce; I just need to sleep it off," Foster protested.

Without a word, an obviously upset Kenneth went back to Mr McEnuff's, leaving the chatter behind; he had strong suspicions about the perpetrators. It was the first time anything like this happened in Macca Tree, and so the usually quiet neighborhood erupted in panic at the sight of a decrepit Foster. With the news spreading like wild fire that Foster was hijacked and beaten at Mr McEnuff's house, Top and Bottom roads residents came forth as well; even Pastor and Monica were in the midst offering comfort to the family.

Heading up the spine to Mr McEnuff's, the street lights were Kenneth's only company, as everyone else was heading in the opposite direction towards Foster. Walking past trees and shrubs, he suddenly became very aware of what had happened, as his adrenaline wore off and fear set in; indigestion formed in the pit of his stomach and soon negative frightening thoughts joined the unrest. Within the confines of his own logics, Kenneth felt an obligation to Mr McEnuff to see what was missing from the property.

With each step, his heart was pounding faster, but that was not enough to deter him.

The banana leaves formed images of people in the slight breeze in the dead of night. In a mad rush, Kenneth fell to his knees, crawling in the grass. Engulfed by fear, noises in the nearby bushes startled him to sit in a fetal position, hugging his legs to his chest. Sitting there for a while Kenneth was paralyzed, feeling like he was sitting on pins and needles. Realizing that it was dancing shadows, he got a grip, but wished for a drink to drown the illusions. Still, he wondered what would happen if the thieves were really Tiger and Cheddy and even worse, what would happen if they were still on the farm. Now trapped in his brain, Kenneth regretted the decision. But he was too close to turn back, so he entered the house.

The night was seemingly as hot as the day when he entered the residence, as sweat washed his body and soaked his clothes. Confused by his own brain, Kenneth thought it was about midnight. Looking around at the ransacked dining room, he realized that paintings were torn down and the impeccable room he once had breakfast in was now unrecognizable. Still, he knew not what was taken. Lost in the rubble of misfortune he knew the best thing to do was call Mr McEnuff first, then the police. Resolving to do so, he locked the doors and left.

The crowd still had not dispersed when he got back to Foster. In fact, it had grown bigger. Spending about half an hour there, Kenneth listened as Foster retold the story countless times, revelling in the attention. But Gloria never showed her face in that crowd and was inside her house with the children, except for Ken. Assuming he was in the crowd outside, Kenneth went back on his verandah where he tried to clear his head. Soon, thereafter, he fell asleep.

Sneaking past him that night, Gloria masterfully made no noise. Using only night-time to contact Monica was now a routine that even the dogs expected, barking at her advances and retreats. Not passing Tiger and Cheddy that night was the only detail out of place, but Gloria hurried on her way as due to the earlier happenings, their meeting had to be pushed to a later time. Now at 11:00 p.m., she waited on Monica to emerge from the doorway. Within minutes, Monica was on her way to Gloria in the pit-black of night.

As the women exchanged quick greetings, a third voice emerged from the dark.

"Don't make anodder sound, and if any a oonu move one more step, the two a unoo dead tonight."

Masked men – two of them – appeared from nowhere. Each held one of the women, covering their mouths with hands that smelled of pig manure. Gloria swooned instantly.

"Don't mek a sound," one of the men reminded an apparently comatose Monica.

Their resistance took flight in the fright of the moment. Both women nodded in complete submission. So the men freed their mouths.

"Just gi wi di money and wi won't hurt yuh!"

"Which money, sar? Wi don't know what yuh talking about. I is a woman of God. How dare you come on mi property and harass mi?" Monica rediscovered her temerity.

"Lady, yuh mad to bring God inna dis. Just gi wi di money wha unoo a mek down at the church and wi won't tek yuh life."

"Which money? I already tell yuh wi have none," Monica argued.

Reviving, a dazed Gloria gathered her thoughts.

"Wi not going to ask yuh again whey di money deh," the man who had kept silent up to this time, spoke. "Wi just a go go inside and tek it."

"You wouldn't dare..." was all Monica could get out before a slime-filled rag was stuffed into her mouth and the bile in her stomach rushed up to meet it. A greasy piece of rope secured her hands behind her. She started to choke on her own vomit. With a crocus bag placed over her head, Monica shook on the ground as though Spirit-possessed. A quiet Gloria gasped, swallowed hard and stared with bulging eyes as one of the men entered the house with an empty bag while the other held her firmly to the ground with an evil, watchful gaze. Inside, Pastor saw the man and started to raise an alarm, a hard slap silenced him. A groan was followed by a loud thud as the body of the anointed one, cloth and all, hit the floor. Unsure of whether or not the thief was armed, Monica kept still. Gloria tried nothing. It was a conspiracy of silence that had served all of them, one from which none dared break free, even to save their own lives.

"Why yuh doing this?" Gloria asked finally.

"Lady, mi nuh haffi tell yuh nutten. And if yuh gwaan talk, mi put a bag over yuh head to," the man said. Looking around in the dark, Gloria could see movement and a form; she realized it was actually three men, but the third remained hidden.

Emerging from the house, the thief exited with a full bag; Gloria's captor, seeing him, got up and ran behind him scaling the picket fence like an athlete. The third man joined them as they disappeared down the road. Gloria ran over to Monica, taking the cloth from her mouth.

"Bawl fi teef Gloria. Stop dem!" Monica shouted.

Jumping up to awaken the community on the heels of the robbery, Gloria quickly held her tongue as she tried to make out the silhouette of the third masked thief. He was strangely familiar. His face was undisclosed, but his frame was a giveaway. She closed her eyes and with that single movement, she also closed her mind. It was just not possible.

18. Whodunit

If one looked in the dictionary for the words chaos and confusion, disbelief and distrust, anger and ambiguity, high resolution pictures of Monica and Gloria seated on the ground covered in dew would emerge.

"Call fi teef, Gloria," Monica insisted.

Dumfounded, Gloria looked at her.

"Gloria, Gloria…"

But, for Gloria, all was still. She didn't even hear the mongrels yapping at the men creating a raucous in retreat.

Hyperventilating, she did not know how to extricate herself from the cocoon of horror that had encased her. Her world was on fast-forward. Gloria found herself slowing down to motionlessness. Clasping her trembling hands so tightly, she did not even feel the wedding band cutting into her flesh. This could not be, she thought.

Her emotions in a knot tried to stifle her and when they failed, they attempted to strangle her instead. Shame rolled down Gloria's face in uncontrollable tears as she tried to figure out how and why this had happened.

"Gloria, a yuh carry in man pon wi?" Monica's voice was full of incredulity.

"What… why mi wudda do that, Monica?" Gloria asked, unsure of everything.

"Because yuh is teef just like di last time when yuh take di people dem money."

Just then, the pastor stumbled out and untied Monica's hands.

"Monica is what going on?" he asked.

"Pastor, Gloria carry in teef pon wi. Mek I go check the money." With that, she ran to the house and came back in short order hollering.

"Dat's why yuh neva want di money go a bank. Yuh did want tell dem fi come take all of it!"

"What yuh mean, Monica? All di money gone?" A still-incoherent Gloria asked.

"Di man dem what you send take all of it!" Monica shouted. Running on to the streets, Monica stirred a commotion by bawling out: "teef!"

Dressed in a black see-through nightgown, Monica transformed into the virago she had long ago hidden beneath the holy charade.

She sought no resolve from Gloria, who ran behind her begging her to stop and declaring her innocence. Behind them the pastor trailed in his underpants and T-shirt.

"Monica, please," Gloria shouted, "let mi talk to yuh. Is not mi, I swear, Monica!" Gloria tried fruitlessly to keep up.

"Yuh think mi is a fool, Gloria? If is no yuh, then is who? Yuh not pinning this one on mi. No sah! Teef!"

By now, Monica had awoken all of Top Road and Macca Tree. Unable to keep up with her, Gloria fell behind, panting. By the time she got to Macca Tree, there was a crowd assembled in the front of her house, with Monica in the middle.

"Unoo let har back in and this is what she do. She teef from unoo, again!" Monica shouted.

"No!" Gloria shouted, joining the crowd and seeing a worried Kenneth. With his hand held out in a questioning position, Gloria could only shrug in response while shaking her head saying no.

"Please, unoo listen to mi. I don't ask any a unoo fi nutten, but I asking yuh to listen to me this one time. I never tek unoo money. Monica lying."

"Yuh have di gall fi ask us fi believe yuh, Gloria? After all yuh put us through?" Dolly asked.

At that moment, Gloria realized that she had no cards to play. She was among savages, and, by experience, she knew what they were capable of. Hiding behind their kaleidoscope houses and the church, she knew the residents concealed their hearts, but their reasoning when joined together in such fashion was always unmistaken.

Gloria's world began to spin out of control and her words were as heavy as the boulders in the community. Shutting down reason which made no sense in the face of current reality, Gloria tried to talk. Scared of the very words she would mention, even the saliva on her tongue failed to aid the process.

"What yuh have to say for yourself, Gloria?" Joyce asked. "Speak now! The last time yuh teef it was from wi in Macca Tree. Now you teef from di entire Westmoreland. Bwoy, I tell yuh, neighbours, once a teef, always a teef." She riled them up instantly. But Kenneth saw what was happening again and spoke up.

"Joyce, gi har a chance mek she talk nuh," he finally said.

He was shut up instantly with a threat from Joscelyn. Kenneth was still unsure of what was going on, but this was his wife. And, until they could prove she had done something unspeakable, he would defend her. The last time Gloria was in a pickle with Macca Tree, it was because she had done something to save her mother's life. If Gloria had taken money again, he knew it would be for something honourable to someone.

Not backing down this time Kenneth said, "Don't talk to mi like that, Joscelyn. I tired of unoo accusing us. Mek she talk. Gloria was yuh friend, Dolly. Yuh kick har when she was down and yuh want to do it again. You, Darcy, is mi bredda, and yuh neva tek di time fi find out what did really happen. But this time, unoo will listen to har before unoo judge har. Monica, yuh need to stop hiding behind the church wid yuh wicked self. That's yuh cousin, have har back this time. She is no teef more than yuh; at least she not pretending to be something she not!"

Dumfounded, everyone was silent. Too much was happening all at once and at the wrong time of day. In the moment, a proud Ken walked up to his father and stood beside him as though he was the only person that mattered in the world. Nodding at Ken as though they had an understanding, Kenneth looked back at Gloria and said, "Talk, Gloria."

Clearing her throat and taking the scarlet letter from her chest, Gloria began to speak. Being in the centre of the mob, she turned momentarily to speak to everyone personally.

"People of Macca Tree, I owe unoo an apology. Yes, I did tek unoo money last time. Mi mother had cancer and I couldn't afford di bills. So I took unoo pardna money to help har."

Murmurs erupted and Monica stepped back into the crowd. Gloria continued to talk.

"I left, and unoo gave mi a chance to come back. I came back vex because this was mi home and unoo throw mi out like I was nutten. I felt like a dog."

Still they said nothing.

"I came back with a plan. I wanted to buy back all I did own and I wanted to show unoo that I could make unoo get back more than I did take from unoo too. So I told Monica about 'planting a seed' and she told unoo about it in church."

Everyone turned to look at Monica, but she was gone. Slipped from their clutches like the snake she represented. Pastor was still in the crowd and received the dirtiest stares on his wife's behalf.

"I told har to keep di money at har yaad, because she would have to answer too much questions if she did carry it to bank. I went to see har since night to discuss di way forward and some man just come from nowhere and rob us."

"Yuh know is who, Gloria?" Dolly asked. "Because I want back every red cent."

Before Gloria could respond, Kenneth stepped in.

"Well it is a night of robbery, because dem beat up Foster earlier and take Mr McEnuff key and try fi rob his place too. I was trying to keep this until we could get the police here tomorrow, but we better call the police now before anything else happen."

Joyce chimed in, "Call the police now, 'cause Foster won't tell mi what happen. Him still beat up and in pain, and nobody really know what going on."

Then Kenneth went silent. He was unwilling to accuse anyone without proof and Foster had provided none.

Gloria looked around at everyone. At this point, even nature quieted. There were no roosters crowing in the wee hours beckoning to the morning. No crickets whistled in the grass, no frogs croaked, no dogs barked, no one spoke, and even the wind's jaws seemed to have frozen shut.

Kenneth walked over to Gloria and held her hands.

"Glor, if yuh saw who robbed Pastor's house, tell wi. It must be the same ones who rob Mr McEnuff and beat up Foster. "Tell mi is who, Glor," he urged.

Whispering in Kenneth's ear, the crowd watched as his eyes bulged at what Gloria told him.

"Yuh sure, Gloria? That nuh sound right!" he shouted.

Looking around at the crowd, Kenneth himself was now speechless. But then his voice found favour with his vocal chords. "I did not trust dem strangers him bring into the place." He said to himself.

"Trust who? Which strangers? Who bring strangers Kenneth?" Joyce was adamant: "Unoo talk now... yuh know, because we will limb dem up and hang dem out until the police come!"

The men in the crowd looked at each other. They too had been wondering about the two strange men working on the McEnuff farm and who lingered along the roadway at nights. And Kenneth's words were not lost on them.

19. Fall of the Bourgeois

These were serious times. Like a partner to mystery, nature picked up where it left off before the hush; an elusive night breeze drifted slowly through the community. The cool fresh air carried distress and despair, even as it offered peace, quiet and solace. But instead of nightingales and hooting owls giving voice to the night, the entire community of Macca Tree was awake; sleep evaporated from their eyes and launched them into a fully fledged hunt for two men fitting the description of Tiger and Cheddy.

The hunt took them into the wee hours of the morning and landed them back at the wrought-iron automated gates.

"So, Maas Kenneth, what yuh suggest wi duh?" Joyce asked.

Taken aback by the role into which he has been thrust, Kenneth put on his stern face and tried to take charge of the situation. The respect he had so long crave had finally come.

"Mek wi look fi dem again," he said. "Dem can't gone too far; is one way into Macca Tree and one way out."

"Careful, Kenneth, don't mek dem hurt yuh," Gloria warned.

Kenneth and the able-bodied men armed themselves with machetes, hoes and sticks and headed out, combing the community for Tiger and Cheddy.

With the wind on their backs making air pillows of their shirts, dried leaves, dampened with the night's dew flew like confetti in the fresh breeze. Kenneth, the man of the moment, was large and in charge. He walked confidently with a pronounced swagger, pulling the fresh breeze deep into his lungs, exhaling loudly. Nature, in full acknowledgment of the return of his manhood, had found its life in the dead of night.

Time passed. No result. Stars hiding themselves told the moon to hurry along as it lingered waving a slow, smiling goodbye, taking the secrets of the night with it, as the sun began its peak over the hillside. The orange glow streaked across the horizon while patches of clouds, still carrying the dark outline of the passing night, dragged themselves out of the way. The birds joined the search from above, circling the community as if on watch.

Rendezvousing in front of the McEnuff's house, the group plotted their next move. By this time, the women had retired to making breakfast the Macca Tree way, so their victors could feast when they returned with the men and the money. Pastor still had not gone home, but remained in the midst, lost in every which way. Tossing a piece of wood to him, Joscelyn was shocked to see him succumb to the weight and buckle. The pastor, frail and afraid, had become the comedic relief in a very sinister play.

"So, what now Kenneth?" Joscelyn asked.

"Well, there is only one more place to look," Kenneth said.

In a synchronized movement, all looked towards Tom McEnuff's house. Suddenly, the pillar of the community lost its splendour and exceptionality. "Mek wi go look if Tom house a harbour criminals," he added.

"Well, is him bring di thief dem into Macca Tree. Maybe dem hiding over there."

Leading the charge to Mr McEnuff's, Kenneth felt good to be on this side for a change. Up to that point, he did not tell anyone about the actual break-in at the big house. He wanted to talk to Mr McEnuff first, himself. But he could find no reason why a search could not be conducted of the farmlands. Just, maybe, finding Tiger and Cheddy will solve all the robberies in one fell swoop, he thought to himself.

As the leader of a rebellion against persons who came into his community and tried to steal from the hard-working people of Macca Tree without good reason, Kenneth had found a cause. He could act with good explanation. Upon examining the gate in front of them, the men realized that it had to be forced open as Foster was robbed of the keys and as far as they knew, Tom McEnuff was still in Kingston.

Before Kenneth could devise a plan, Joscelyn had charged at it with his pickaxe stick. The gate gave way after the sudden onslaught of the stick and a push by two of the men.

The group rushed on to the property shouting the names of the criminals they pursued. They did not reach far on the property when Tom McEnuff emerged, wearing a white shirt, a pair of jeans and black and white two-toned gentleman's shoes, partly covered in red mud. He raised his hand to stop the startled men in their tracks. Without a word, he pointed towards a sign that hung loosely from the bend iron of the gate: 'Trespassers will be prosecuted'.

"What the hell is wrong with unoo? I leave here Kenneth with you in charge and come back to see my place ransacked! What the hell is going on! Unoo come through mi gate, tearing it down like wild animals! I calling the police on the whole of unoo right now!" Tom McEnuff was enraged.

Kenneth was shocked beyond belief. He dropped the machete and the leadership role all at once.

"Mr Mack, I would never steal from yuh. I respect yuh too much, I wanted to be like yuh, but I wouldn't steal to be you. I was waiting on you to come back to tell you that man come on the property and beat up Foster and take away yuh key and entered yuh house. I did not want to raise an alarm in the community 'cause I did not want anyone to come over here and trouble anything else. I swear, Mr Mack, I swear!"

Foster limped forward. But he did not get a word in edgewise.

"Get off mi property before I call the police," Tom said.

"Call them, Mr Mack, because wi want dem to come. Wi have tiefs here in Macca Tree and wi want di police come find dem!" Joscelyn shouted.

"So, why you think them up here? You forgetting your place Kenneth. I made you. You living in my doghouse, you work for me, cleaning my sty. Now yuh think I am harbouring thieves in mi yard?"

"Yes, Mr Mack. Yuh harbouring tiefs. Wi never trust di man dem what yuh carry come here; now dem rob from the community and yuh haffi answer fi dat. So wey dem deh?" Ken said.

"Where is Tiger and Cheddy, Mr Mack?" Kenneth regained his composure. "Where is the bwoy dem who come rob the place, the same ones who yuh bring and you did not know anything bout dem."

No one could have guessed that a day would come when Tom McEnuff had to answer to Kenneth Mann. The community men stood back waiting for Mr Mack to respond, waiting to be summoned into action by Kenneth, who had edged closer to Tom.

Once the most beautiful place on earth to Kenneth, the plantation now reeked of robbery and deceit, overnight.

Retrieving a pack of cigarettes from his pocket, Kenneth lit one and fixed his gaze on Mr McEnuff. He pulled in deeply. The air was no longer fresh, but it soothed his lungs. Flicking off the ashes, he took another draw of the butt, "Wi waiting, sar."

With all eyes on Tom, neither Kenneth nor his back-up men saw Gloria sneaking on to the property.

She kept her distance in the shadowy dim of the early-morning light; she bit her tongue, maintaining her stillness. Her eyes drifted to Tom McEnuff. He was still wearing the shoes and jeans she had identified at Pastor's earlier, when he darted from the bushes as the third man in the band of thieves.

That black and white pair of gentleman's shoes made him take boasty steps throughout Macca Tree; but the mileage on his shoes did not show because of how well kept it was. That scary pair of shoes was such a part of Mr McEnuff, glued to his feet whenever he was not in his combat boots. Now, for Gloria, it formed a part of the horror that was the night before, as the shoes, with its muddied sole, gave up its owner.

Gloria made her way through the bushes like a slithering snake and headed towards the shed at the back of the house. The shed hosted the wheelbarrows, tools and the secrets of the McEnuffs; Kenneth had mentioned that the workers were never allowed to venture into its sacred space. Gloria kept her cool and looked around. Finally reaching the shed, she found that, as luck would have it, the door was unlocked. The padlock hung like a suspended pendulum from its saddle; she disappeared inside. Stacks of animal feed lined the walls. The smell of old newspaper and animal dung permeated the atmosphere. A bundle of loose crocus bags was thrown down in one corner.

She moved quickly to the bundle. At the bottom of the pile, her hand moved across the treasured lump. She had hit jackpot. Tom McEnuff did not get enough time to secure the stolen money. She took up the crumpled sack and headed out of the shed. She did not return to the front yard, but took the bushes at the back of the building. Gloria scaled the fence that led to her house like an athlete. She took the stash to a hole she had dug in the ground and covered it with wild bush, securing it with a boulder she had rolled in place.

In the McEnuff front yard, Kenneth continued his cold staring down of his former boss.

"Mr Mack, wi have a feeling yuh know about what the two vagabond of a man yuh bring come around here...."

Tom McEnuff had reached the end of his tether.

"Kenneth, I will not stand for yuh disrespecting me like this. Yuh have the temerity to talk to me like that in front of these men, after you and Foster break into mi place."

Finally, Foster found his voice.

"Tom McEnuff, yuh bring two man into the place and yuh don't tell nobody who dem be. Well, dem beat me up, and take away yuh key and go inno yuh house. Is the same two man dem that tief the church money from Gloria and Monica. Yuh can't blame me and Kenneth for the actions of yuh own man dem. Call di police, Mr Mack, 'cause we want to talk to dem to."

Mr McEnuff stuttered a response. "Alright, I really did not lose much. They break a few picture frames, but all in all, everything is still intact. Let me get mi gun and help with the search." He volunteered.

Kenneth took back control. "But call the police first. Two wrongs don't make a right. We don't want to find them, 'cause man and man will kill them. Make the police do dem job. Call de police."

Tom hesitated for a second. "I can't tell the police about the money from the plan, because it is a Ponzi scheme and it not legal here."

The men looked confused.

"What yuh saying, McEnuff?" Kenneth quizzed. "Yuh did know dat the plan was illegal and yuh said nothing?"

He opened his mouth as if to speak, then changed his mind, turned and walked into his great room and picked up the phone.

Tom spoke in hushed tones, but the men could hear him giving the description of Tiger and Cheddy. Then he returned to the group.

"The superintendent said we are to leave this matter to the long arm of the law and you must go home. He said di bwoys are hardened criminals and they have them on their watch list and they are likely to be armed and dangerous. So, unoo call off the search and just leave my property and go to unoo yard."

The men whispered among themselves. The possibility of not getting back their money hit home hard. Silent, confused and heavy-hearted, they turned and walked towards the iron gate.

"Wi will leave yuh to yuhself now, but as soon as di police hold dem, make sure dem have the money. Wi want back wi money, even if it illegal." Joscelyn clung to the fading hope as if his life depended on it.

The men retreated to their yards. As the sun established its dominance over the morning, the now unusual smell of roast breadfruit and fried dumplings retook its place in the Macca Tree atmosphere. The sound of 'broomweed' on the asphalt echoed in the distance. Someone was sweeping the street.

20. The Great Clean-up

In the days that followed, the police were still hot on the trail of Cheddy and Tiger. Clues took them to Savanna-la-Mar where talk was heavy about excessive spending by the two men. They followed leads to Negril, where the lawmen descended on the resort town. It was indeed another hot summer day; it was one of those days one often heard about when an egg could be fried on a sidewalk. The sun had spread an orange velvety blanket over the earth that not even the wind could challenge. Still, it was a beautiful tropical day for the five undercover cops patrolling the beach, looking for the suspects.

Endless and white, the extremely soft sand begged them to stay a while, clinging to their feet, demanding slow steps. But the heat on their soles was too much, and fearing blood blisters they stopped under some coconut trees for a while. They looked on amidst the blinding glare of the sun on the sand and saw on the horizon that even the boats were basking, bobbing to the rise and fall of the powerful turquoise waves. A few black clouds threatened to stain the blue sky, proving the weatherman was right the night before when he predicted rain.

With not much time before the downpour, the officers walked on. Going around the obstacles of beach chairs, umbrellas, children playing with shells and adults relaxing on towels, locals and tourist alike, they carefully manoeuvred so as not to miss their intended targets. Then, there was Tiger and Cheddy; spotted on the beach; sprawled out on lounge chairs, donning floral trunks, heavily laden in gold chains and too-large pendants, drinking clear liquid from miniature-umbrella-adorned wine glasses. They were oblivious to their emerging captors.

Sitting in front of a small shack selling fried fish and festival, they gave each other high fives, whistling in appreciation as scantily clad women passed by. The officers, dressed also in beachwear, moved in on them swiftly. Signalling to the shop owner to turn down a recording of Beenie Man's 'Girls Dem Sugar', they swooped in. The officers were sure of their identification because the thieves called each other by name. Surrounding them, they were taken in shock and awe, declaring their innocence as the handcuffs were easily snapped in place.

"Cheddy Chambers and Tigara Pottinger, we are police officers and we have been looking for you guys for a while now.'"

"Looking for wi for what, sar?" they both asked startled, starting to get up.

"Well, you guys are very notorious, but most recently, you are both suspects in robberies in the Macca Tree community; now we just want to take you in for questioning."

"For what, sar, wi never duh nothing," Cheddy said.

"Well, then you have nothing to fear; just come with us to the station. We will clear up everything there."

The men were searched, and a bag which was on the ground near to where they were sitting was identified as theirs by the bartender. The bag was also searched and a fully loaded Smith and Wesson firearm was found hidden beneath clothes and a wad of cash. Tiger immediately named Cheddy as the owner of the firearm. His accusation was met with Cheddy's who declared that he knew nothing about the weapon.

"Check di finger print pon di gun!" Cheddy hollered. "Only di owner touch it!" he wailed.

Tiger said nothing, but stared at his accomplice in disbelief.

"Yuh let me down bad, Cheddy." Tiger uttered. "Mi never expect yuh fi cave in so quickly."

Hissing his teeth, Cheddy replied, "Just stop di talking man; yuh only a go mek things worse."

The men were escorted from the beach under the eyes of tourists and locals alike.

"You are both under arrest for the robberies in Macca Tree." One of the officers announced, hoping to answer the quizzical stares that followed the group.

Trying to drum up support, Cheddy cried for police brutality, but no one moved in his defence. As they were leaving the beach, the music returned to its deafening decibel and everyone returned to their previous activity.

"So yuh real name is Tigara? No wonder yuh call yuhself Tiger," Cheddy said while they walked back to the police jeep.

"Nuh worry 'bout my name, worry bout whether or not Mr McEnuff a go come bail wi."

"Well, him don't have a choice now, does he?" Cheddy asked.

But Tom McEnuff had a choice; the choice of money. Walking into the Savanna-la-Mar Police Station that night, he oozed power and authority. It was that power and authority that both Tiger and Cheddy respected, feared and wanted for themselves. Walking up to the inspector, Tom shook his hand, had a little chat with him and then was escorted inside. Walking to the back of the station, the fresh air left Tom McEnuff's nostrils, replaced by a stale rancid odour. Their cell was small and sleeping area dishevelled. In there every idea of freedom and privacy evaporated. The floor was bare concrete and the ceiling fan over their heads made a continuous noise when it moved, which kept everyone awake. The cream paint on the wall gave way to the grey on the ceiling, creating a deliberately drab ambience. As he walked through, the light flicked on and off, but Tom was able to see the spring bed on which they would lay their heads that night, no doubt the sheets were dirty because that awful smell had to originate somewhere. He faced his accomplice and foes in the same moment, in the same bodies. Both men were eagerly awaiting his arrival.

"It's OK, you can leave," he told the officer who stood guard. "I just want to have a word with these low grades. They can do no more harm; after all they are behind bars." Returning to his desk further out, the officer resumed doing some paperwork.

"Wi neva mention yuh name if that's what yuh asking!" Cheddy quickly spoke up.

Tom placed his finger over his lips, signalling their silence.

"So what now? Yuh gonna bail wi or what?" Tiger asked.

"Well, you guys have never been caught before. Now that you have, I have to fire you. I came because there was a report that you broke into my property and out of respect, the inspector gave me a chance to confront you both. So, here I am, confronting the criminals who stole from mi."

"But a you tell wi fi do that," Tiger said.

"What! Why would I tell you to do any such thing? You are two wicked men. Imagine, I take you on my farm and give you work and you turn around and steal from me, and then go and rob the people in the community! Dem should get together and limb unoo up!" Tom McEnuff was enraged.

His outburst brought back the inspector to the cell.

The rusty metal bars that separated the men from Tom McEnuff were not as cold as him. Looking at him in disbelief, Tiger and Cheddy knew they were going to prison.

Disbelief turned into deep sorrow.

Stepping back, Mr McEnuff continued calmly, "Look, where is the money that you took last night?"

"What money?" Cheddy asked.

Tiger chimed in, "We never take all of the money. We took some and left the rest in yuh barn. Make the police search yuh barn. The money deh deh." He snarled.

"You expect me to believe that? Two criminals telling me that the money you stole is in my shed? Well I never...."

The Inspector stepped in.

"Mr Mack, come now, sar. I will send a team to check yuh shed. We need some fingerprints from your property as well."

He nodded sheepishly and left with the officer.

The McEnuffs' main house and shed were brushed for fingerprint evidence and Tiger and Cheddy had left their marks all over the compound, on the wall plaques, on the lamp in the great room and on the crocus bags in the shed. Since they were not allowed to go into the house or the shed, their fingerprints being there provided evidence enough to charge them with the crime. The fact that Tom McEnuff's own prints were also detected did not add him to the list of suspects, being the owner of the property; his had a right to be there. No money was found in the shed.

When charges were laid against Tiger and Cheddy, they steered clear of mentioning their former boss, and so he was never officially linked or charged in the robbery; his secret was buried along with the God plan in Macca Tree.

But, in the dark crevice of his mind, guilt would not leave Tom McEnuff unscathed. He decided to compensate the residents by committing an undisclosed sum to the church. He explained to Pastor that he was at fault for bringing Tiger and Cheddy to Macca Tree and he felt moved to pay for his mistake. Since no one knew exactly how much was stolen, nobody complained about the size of the donation; but many made a final attempt to benefit from the God plan by going to the church to collect. Those outside Macca Tree

- Top Road and Bottom Road - lost their investment, but the three communities, as if in a conspiracy, remained quiet about their compensation; for all everyone else knew, the money was stolen, never recovered and the men responsible were in prison.

Half of Westmoreland showed up for the sentencing of the thieves, hurling degrading comments at them as they were led from the docks, guilty as charged and sentenced to ten years each, at hard labour.

"How unoo fi rob from poor people?"

"How unoo fi rob from God?"

"How unoo so wicked? Wi want justice!"

The people shouted.

But the Macca Tree residents felt somewhat reprieved by the outcome, though the fences with Tom McEnuff were never mended. They were vehement in their belief that good trumps evil, and that justice was served.

In celebration of their refund, the residents of Macca Tree decided to 'run a boat' and invited their Top Road and Bottom Road neighbours to join in. The road was abuzz with activities, and laughter rang out loud. Chased by autumn, summer was retreating and it was a cool day; ridding itself of the scourge that was, the community delighted in the chilling air, which smelled of damp earth. Mary showed up with pastries such as grater cake and gizzardas, drops and ducunoos, coloured puffs and potato puddings in big woven straw baskets.

Dolly helped Joyce make her famous manish water soup, flavoured by one of Joscelyn's ram goats, in a big pot at her gate. The popping of the logwood sent sparks into the blue skies as smoke escaped the dancing flames. Children played cricket and danced in the cleanly swept road and the spirit of Macca Tree was returning slowly but surely.

Not to be left out of the celebration, Kenneth and Gloria roasted fish, stuffed with callaloo and spices in a drum-pan placed horizontally and full of slow-burning charcoal. The usual fried chicken with rice and peas that perfumed the area on a Sunday afternoon was there that Saturday, luring all, except Tom McEnuff.

Having fired Kenneth and given him notice to leave his property, Tom had become Macca Tree's enemy and a near recluse. The day's merriment ended well, with the usual antics of Foster, the undisputed community clown. Re-enacting his beat down, he showed off with wacky movements what had happened, or at least what he could remember. The togetherness of the community was again intact, and although it was Gloria's idea that had taken them on a turbulent journey, it was Kenneth's action that took them back to a place of rest.

21. Macca Tree's Rebirth: The Manns' Redemption

The Macca Tree residents accepted that the theft was God's punishment for their abandonment of His principles. They had been forcefully reminded that you cannot plant corn and reap peas. Sewing and reaping had been their lot, yet they had hoped to reap interest from seeds they did not sew.

Pastor's message was powerful that last Sunday under the big tent.

"The Lord is vexed wid wi. Our parents send wi to Sunday school to learn what is right and what is proper. We learn long time that by the sweat of our brows we will eat bread Sweating in lines to invest in a plan cannot reap us any good. What appears to be of God was of the enemy himself. The love of money still is the root of all evil!" Pastor was on a tirade and the congregation grunted at each point of punctuation.

The revival crusade was to be the spiritual cleansing of the community and to purify the remnants of the God plan. Vowing never to allow anything to rip them apart again or blind them from God's grace and goodness, they heeded to the words of their pastor.

"You see, brethren, God tests us but never leaves us, no, no, no; he waits to reward us once the lesson is learnt. So if you have learnt your lesson, can I get a witness?" Pastor shouted as the hands were raised one by one.

Amens and hallelujahs disrupted the voice of Pastor as he tried to continue over the din. He was silenced into his own mumblings as the congregation was moved by the Spirit.

Some found a place at the crowded altar, kneeling and weeping away their sorrow, regret and guilt.

Others, in too-high volumes, were inviting God back to Macca Tree, declaring that they will stand against evil in the years to come.

Monica, who was seated on a hard board bench at the back of the gathering, looked on in silence. She kept her head bowed, and her face held the glare of regret and pious repentance. She, however, did not escape the stares and glances of hatred that once belonged to Gloria.

The back bench was hers, even after she bellowed an apology in confession. It was easier for the church to accept Gloria who they thought was fooled by the devil while in the world, than Monica who blatantly played God while holding such high office in church.

Pastor was forgiven because the congregation knew him and knew he would not be a part of any plan to swindle them of their hard-earned cash. But they did not know Monica. She was easily relegated to the position of stranger in the district she had come to call home. Monica was Pastor's wife, but she was not Pastor, and he was not willing to give up his flock to stand by the side of the community swindler, at least not by day, even if he must by night.

As the faithful danced and sang their praises, Joyce grabbed the microphone from a befuddled Pastor and ordered the congregation into single file, leading a march through the community.

The congregation, daring not to upset the flow of the Spirit took their place behind Joyce, who loudly tracked the words of the old hymn 'Onward Christian Soldiers' as they walked to the rhythm.

The congregation stopped briefly at the newly installed automatic gate of the McEnuff property, with its updated security feature and freshly painted signs – 'Keep out!', 'Beware of Dogs', 'Trespassers will be shot!'

In defiance, the choir launched into a musical assault belting out songs and psalms amidst a barrage of unknown tongues. Gloria, who had now found a place of acceptance among the flock took full aim at the unresponsive gate with her words.

"Tom give yuh heart to the Lord, He is the way, the truth and the light, Tom!" she shouted. "Yuh money cyaa save yuh, Tom..."

But Tom McEnuff never came out to see them and from where they stood they had to contend with his newly acquired barking pit bulls and opera music which grew by volumes once they arrived. With no one looking after his acres of farmland, the once flourishing property was now like a desert – parched and dry. Not even his house seemed like the oasis it once was. He had lost his respectability and his shine. He had sold out much of his livestock. Driven by shame, his trips to Kingston to his wife became more frequent and now, like her, no one knew when he was really home. Except for the music that played loudly, there was no sign of life on the property.

Macca Tree farmlands awoke to the revival of spring after the days of woe. Fruit trees began to bud, green leaves started a furious fight to overcome their dried-up counterparts and grass that had withered and turned brown under the blazing sun were showing green at the roots.

Wind puffed up with the sweet stench of fertilizer swayed the assortment of fruits trees, laden with buds and young fruits. The swamp in Bottom Road once again was swollen from the last shower of rain and wells with mosquito-infested water. Wide open spaces were showing sprouts of weeds and mangrove. The hillsides were beginning to regain their lustre as the patches of dirt took cover under growing shrubbery.

Freshly washed and wrung clothes danced in the wind on lines strung from tree to poles. Blue skies held no grudges against the community and clouds gave the sun permission to smile brightly at the residents. The sound of water and birds arrested Macca Tree, and like a painting, it reclaimed its place as a lush and vibrant wonderland.

Finding no comfort in the community and the painful silence at home, Monica contemplated a return to Savanna-la-Mar. She could no longer find comfort in her husband, who distanced himself from her in every respect. Gloria, her one-time friend, cousin and accomplice, had not forgiven her for trying to pin the robbery on her that night.

Furthermore, Gloria, Kenneth and the children had moved to Savanna-la-Mar to a house once owned by her late grandmother, which she and Kenneth had renovated on their own after the old woman left to be with the Lord, in the midst of the first Macca Tree crisis.

As one would guess, Gloria was keen on not losing her buried plunder of five hundred, one thousand and five thousand dollar bills she had rescued from Tom McEnuff's shed. Stepping out in the chilling morning air as an early bird to catch a big worm, she had dug up the once buried treasure and carefully tucked the bag inside a box and put the box in the oven. Bounded with duct tape, that crocus bag held her secret closely like it had made a pact with its captor. Using stockings and rope to bind the stove, it was moved with the rest of their belongings to Savanna-la-Mar. There she placed the loot securely in an old trunk her grandmother had kept under a mahogany bed that had been passed from generation to generation. Gloria told Kenneth that she had a little money left from her investment in the God plan, but gave him no more information.

The couple travelled to Macca Tree twice per month to attend church. Gloria and the children were always neatly dressed and they had found full acceptance in the community. Ken, Ron and Tamar were enrolled in school. The primary and junior high schools in Savanna-la-Mar were good places for the children and Gloria positioned herself on the board of the parent-teachers association. She was respectable now in the capital and she could relax and hold up her head.

Kenneth was able to set up his farm at the back of the house and had got himself three pigs, a few goats and was well on his way to purchasing a bull and a heifer.

The absence of friendships and the coldness of a marriage on the rocks, forced Monica to think and do the improbable. She packed her clothes in a bag and moved in quietly, under the cover of darkness into the old, cob-webbed, dilapidated shack that once was the home of the Manns. With an absent Tom McEnuff, Monica simply gave herself permission to invade the otherwise haunting housing. Now even more rundown than before the Manns had moved in, the house should have been demolished; but it held itself up, if for nothing else, just because it too pitied Monica.

Pastor did not stop Monica in her decision to leave him and the manse. He stood by the door and watched as she departed. She was too much trouble and her buxom backside was not worth the bother. Furthermore, members of his flock had already informed him that God had given knowledge that she would not stay in the district. Those who were not so informed worked hard to achieve this.

When Gloria heard of Monica's demise, she was nearly overcome by guilt and at one point opened her mouth to confess to Kenneth. But she quickly regained her senses and took a decision that shocked even herself; she decided to visit Monica.

As she walked up the asphalt road towards the remains of the house, her heart leapt as memories flooded her soul. Monica and Joyce spotted her from different sides of the road.

"What yuh doing here, Gloria?" Joyce asked.

"So I can't come here in the middle of the week, outside of Sunday, Joyce?" she answered her question with a question. "I come to look for Monica; she is still mi cousin, yuh know." Gloria stopped to hug the older woman briefly before walking across the street to Monica who was seated on the wedge of a veranda.

"I lose everything, Gloria, I don't know what to do," she said tearfully.

"Well, all I can do is pray for you," Gloria said, breaking out in unknown tongues.

"So, you mean you never save any of the money; not even a dry-head thousand dollar?" Gloria asked when done.

"No, dem tek everything" Monica said. "Yuh is all mi have."

"So, Pastor allow yuh to leave just like dat?" Gloria asked.

"Him never stop mi. Is me leave. Things get too hard. Mi want to start over. I know God will forgive me, I forgive myself and the people. God will forgive me and restore me one day. But for now, I want to be on my own, and I find it peaceful just right here so," Monica explained.

"Forget the cobweb and the broken-down floor and chip-up walls; this is the place of repentance," she looked at Gloria. "Remember, this is where God took you when He wanted to bring you out."

Gloria looked on in bewilderment.

"Monica, yes, Him bring me here, but Him never change me here. Girl, don't give away yuh life. Go make up wid Pastor and restore yuhself. Here is a little thing I bring for yuh."

Gloria handed her cousin a purse with a few thousand-dollar bills.

Shifting her wig and scratching her head to the amusement of Gloria, she took the purse.

"Well, I must leave now. Just watch out fi di roof on this side; it leak when rain fall. Mind yuh drop through the flooring, but yuh must go back home to yuh husband."

As Gloria made her exit, she shouted back to Monica.

"If yuh going to stay longer, buy some rat poison 'cause yuh a go need nuff a that and it nuh mek sense yuh tear down the cobweb dem, cause by the next day dem a go come back. The only problem with the latrine at the back is the roaches, but yuh know dem harmless."

Monica is left with her memories. Standing at the doorway, she hugged the rotting doorpost as though it was her only company. Watching Gloria leave, she just stood there for a little while. Then she walked into the house, took up the bag that contained her clothes, pulled on a pair of slippers and headed through the wire gate and down the road.

Walking on the clean asphalt over to Foster's, Gloria saw Kenneth in deep conversation. The shiny houses once again stood tall and boasted pride. Gloria was admiring the clean street when her name was called. Looking around, she saw Dolly, Darcy, Joyce and Joscelyn emerging from Dolly's house.

"Di children going up nice, though, Gloria, last time I see dem at Sunday school," Dolly said smiling at the couple.

"T'anks ma'am, I trying mi best," Gloria replied to the older woman. Though she left the gate, Gloria never took her eyes off the old building as she saw her cousin emerge, bag in hand.

"Well, feel free to come and visit us anytime in Sav," she said as she looked past the group.

As she spoke, her mind raced forward to images of grand living spaces she had etched in her mind once the money had started to come in. She pictured herself seated in a plush couch and the group visiting her mansion. Tuning them out, she imagined the setting of the house she still intended to erect: a well-designed living room of positive energy and her playing children; furniture made of carved cedar wood and chairs with armrests of vibrant colour; leather sofas, lavish rugs over exquisite tiles; lace curtains and fancy drapes; large areas of sunlight through a high roof; an open view to a meadow of grazing animals on a blanket of smooth grass and recently planted gungu peas, corn, other vegetables and maybe some sorrel; bathrooms and balconies, a master bedroom with walk-in closet, children's rooms, guest rooms and a big kitchen; sweet river running behind the house and her sitting in a rocking chair with a cup of creamed coffee reading the day's newspaper, across from a sleeping contented Kenneth.

"It is a good feeling to know unoo okay wid wi again." Kenneth interrupted her illusion.

Smiling they continued to look at Gloria, "Well, don't be a stranger now; always member where yuh church membership is. Wi looking to see yuh in church every Sunday," Darcy said.

"Sure, we will be there," she replied. "We can't come every Sunday, but we will come as often as we can."

Walking off from the group, Gloria thought that this is the picture she had hoped for when she returned to Macca Tree, but this is not how she had envisioned it all unfolding. She never intended to be a multi-millionaire so quickly. She didn't know Tom McEnuff and Monica would be reduced to nothing. She didn't know Kenneth would become a man she could once again respect or that she would have got an apology from her former naysayers.

"Kenneth, wi ready," she said to him.

"Alright Glor, I coming," he replied.

Wrapping up his conversation with Foster, Kenneth spoke to him one last time about his pig.

"Yuh know Tom McEnuff give mi dat pig because yuh bounce down Ken; now I have pigs of my own. As soon as I get some piglets, I will bring one come for yuh. I left yuh and yuh get beat up. So this is as Tom did say, my peace offering to you."

Both men laughed.

"Tek care a yuhself, Foster. I will see yuh soon mi frien'," Kenneth said.

"Not if I come look fi yuh first," Foster replied.

Kenneth stepped away from the house, inhaled Macca Tree and then joined Gloria. Indeed, he felt like a man walking down what he still considers to be his road.

"Maas Ken, wi going to miss di roast fish dem," Joyce said.

"Well, wi still near enough to come whenever unoo call, I not dead. Just tell mi when unoo need mi to come roast up a storm." Kenneth laughed

"Wi will definitely tek yuh up on that offer," Joscelyn hailed.

"Kenny, I don't know what to sey. I just sorry about everything. I hope Mama and Papa can forgive mi. I neva stop anything that was happening 'cause I felt yuh deserve it. But I sorry yuh had to go through dat alone," Darcy said.

"Thanks Darcy, but I wasn't alone. I had mi family. I still have dem. Macca Tree will always be a part a wi. Unoo still a go tired fi see wi face," he joked, singing at the end as though he was Bob Marley.

Finally Kenneth and Gloria had freed themselves from the thorny past and sailed smoothly down the spine of the community and out of the glare of their suspicious neighbours.

As they arrived back to their house in Savanna-la-Mar, Gloria's phone was buzzing. Monica was on the other line.

"Gloria, mi husband forgive mi. Him sey him did miss me and wanted to come ask me to come back home, but he was too ashamed. Yuh should a see him when him see me coming up the street. Is like him glad bag bus! Mi call to thank yuh Gloria! If it wasn't for you, I would have stayed in dat godforsaken house of yours! Thank yuh, gal, thank yuh!"

Before Gloria could respond, the line went dead.